The Killing List

by Curtis Walker

The Killing List

To all the victims of stalkers.

Table of Contents

Chapter 1

Dead Man Walking
Friday, January 12, 4:18 PM

Mitch has only three or four months left to live.

Maybe less.

He is dumbfounded. All he can do is stare out in disbelief from the window of Dr. Hussain's 11th-floor office looking out over downtown Winnipeg. A city caught in the grips of another goddamned Arctic air mass that will keep the wind-chill factor below −40 for the next month. Watching the ice fog rise up over the darkening gray sky that is an hour away from plunging the city into total darkness. And cursing under his breath that he will probably not live long enough to see all those piles of snow melt. Piles of snow that are covered in a putrid mixture of frozen vomit and dog piss.

At first, they said it was just migraines. Take two aspirins and call me in the morning. But the aspirins weren't helping. Nor were the extra-strength Tylenols. He tried just about everything. Legal and otherwise. But it was only a temporary escape. Then they sent him for an MRI. Waited months for the appointment. Even though he still didn't think it was that serious, he would have gone to the U.S. and gotten it done much sooner. Except he couldn't afford it anymore. Not to mention that he'd have been turned away at the border because of his record.

At least he was able to go during daylight hours. Not that he felt much safer then than he would have if he had taken the nighttime appointment they first offered him. Those scumbags around the Health Sciences Center present more of a danger than the illness you're going there to get treated for. At any time of the day or night. Sadly par for the course in the violent crime capital of the Western world. One that Mayor McCheese keeps insisting is safe. It's just a perception problem, he says. Just like it was only a perception last fall when that thug in the Polo Park parking lot held a switchblade to Mitch's gut and demanded his wallet. The son of a bitch even went through all his pockets to make sure he wasn't getting short-changed.

It's also just a perception that the cops don't care, says the good-for-nothing police chief. Mitch was just seeing things differently when the lard-ass behind the desk at the District 2 station could barely be bothered to acknowledge his presence when he went in to report the incident after getting out of the urgent care clinic. In between mouthfuls of his double chocolate cream-filled cruller, he just told Mitch to fill out a report online. The asshole didn't even ask if he was OK. Doubt he even noticed the bandages all over his face.

Even though he figured it would be a complete waste of time, he still decided to go through the motions. Except that his Internet service was down again. And yet the repairmen who come out always tell him that no one else in the block has ever had a problem. They say it's only him. The squirrels are only chewing on *his* line. The never-ending problems at the box at the corner only affect *him*. And they can't figure out why. So they say. But Mitch knew why. The phone company was targeting him. He's sure of it. They read the papers. They watch the news. And like everyone else, they believe all the lies. The trumped-up charges. Everything.

It was when Faahima called and asked him to come in right away that he really started getting worried. They don't call you to come in right away unless it's bad. Dr. Hussain said they wanted to do a biopsy by drilling a hole into his skull. Which they did a couple of days later.

As petrified as he was at having a needle probing around inside his brain, waiting for the results was the worst part. It was the most agonizing two weeks of his life. He didn't think Faahima was ever going to get off her ass and call him to come in to review the results. When she finally did call, she blamed the delay on the pathologists. They had to do some extra testing, she said. But he knew she was lying. It only takes seven to 10 days. Maybe less. Especially in a case like this. No, she was sitting on it. Just to make him suffer. He confirmed it when he saw the dates on the form that was lying on her desk when she went to the washroom to fix her babushka. Or whatever they call it in the Middle Eastern shithole country she came from.

As hard as it is to deal with, the bad news almost came as a relief. At least now he knows. He was sick and tired of being a turkey in suspense. Nothing could be worse than that. Nothing. Still, he wonders how can this be? He's only 38. So young. He figured that even if the tumor was malignant, he'd have a better-than-even chance of beating it off. But no, Dr. Hussain said. It was inoperable. It was growing too fast. Radiation would only be able to improve the quality of what little time he had left.

Still sitting in the chair mindlessly stroking the stubble on his salt-and-pepper beard while staring out the window, Dr. Hussain fills him in on how the remaining months of his life will play out. The headaches will get worse. *Jeez, how much worse can they get?* If they get too bad, take it easy, he says. Limit your physical activity. The pain will gradually increase. "I will give you a prescription," Dr. Hussain says. Morphine, Mitch suspects. *That's what everyone seems to get on their deathbed.* He will be more nauseous. He'll likely have seizures. Not like Tourette's. But twitches. Spasms. In time, he could lose some motor skills. He'll have trouble with balance. Then he tells Mitch he has to report it to the Motor Vehicle Branch. They will take away his license, he says. *Fuck that! They're not stopping me from driving! What are they going to do, shoot me?*

Finishing up his canned speech, Dr. Hussain says Mitch will have trouble sleeping. He will also prescribe some sleeping pills. And as the end comes, he will likely need hospice care. Dr. Hussain will put him on a waiting list for Jocelyn House and Grace Hospice. Wherever they can get him in first.

"They will make you as comfortable as possible in your final days."

Finally, Dr. Hussain asks if Mitch has any questions. But he has only one. One that Dr. Hussain can't possibly answer. Even if he wanted to.

Why me?

For the life of him, he just can't understand what he could possibly have done to deserve this. For that matter, why had he seemingly been a victim throughout his life? And not just the rampant antisemitism. That wasn't even the half of it. There were the teachers going back to grade school who kept giving him bad marks and embarrassed him in front of his classmates. His university professors were even worse. They tried to bury him. One of them was so bad Mitch had to drop the course. There was nothing else he could do. Nothing he did was good enough for the old bastard. He thought about filing a grievance with the student union. But when he went to talk to them about it, the bitch started yelling at him and practically threw him out of her office.

There were the bullies in high school who picked on him. And only him. They would constantly steal his lunches. Take his textbooks. Rip up his homework. Spit in his face. Punch him. Kick him in the shins. One of them pushed him to the ground and kicked him so hard he broke two of his ribs. Another hit him in the face and gave him a black eye. And in both cases, they threatened him with much worse if he dared to report it. The teachers knew what was going on, of course. Even the principal saw it for herself once. But none of them would do anything.

It had looked like he would be able to put all that behind him after he graduated. He got a great job, moved up the corporate ladder and soon became the youngest national accounts manager in the company. All while courting his future wife. His soul mate. But it didn't take long before things began falling apart on all fronts. Again. He got screwed over at work, leaving his once-promising career in shambles. And then his wife dumped him like a hot potato. He wasn't good enough for her anymore apparently. But that didn't stop her from taking him to the cleaners. He got hosed so badly it's a wonder he didn't lose his underwear. Clearly, she never really loved him. She just married him because of his family's stature in Winnipeg. He knows that now.

There were others too. It just boggled his mind as to why so many people had it in for him. There was no reason for it. He had always tried to be a good person. Never hurt anyone before. Yet here he was, a victim yet again. It was as if he had been cursed. If only he knew why. That would be the one question he would take to the grave.

But one thing's for sure. Wherever he's going, he's not going alone.

He'll be taking a few others with him.

And he has no time to lose.

Chapter 2

Leah puts down her steaming cup of cinnamon cappuccino on the vintage solid oak table next to her chair in the study and gets up to close the drapes by the bay window. She had opened them earlier so she could wave good bye to Aaron and the kids, who were off to the community club again. She still can't believe they don't cancel those hockey games in this extreme cold. Caleb's game is in the indoor rink, but David's is half an hour later in one of the outdoor rinks.

At least Aaron had been able to finish up with a patient who broke a tooth this afternoon so he could take them. Otherwise, she would have needed to take the kids herself. And she hates driving the Escalade. It's too big. Like a tank. Truth be known, she would have preferred a Jaguar or even another Mercedes to finally fill that last stall in their four-car garage. But they needed the space to fit all that hockey gear. She would probably not hate it so much if Aaron had only picked a different color. Maybe a bright red or light purple. Anything but the satanic black. Next time, she's going with him to the dealer.

Because Aaron had been able to take the boys, it also spared her from having to spend another night shivering in a cold rink sitting on a wooden bench and making small talk with other parents, with her hands wrapped around a Styrofoam cup of lukewarm Carnation hot chocolate. Using the plastic spoon to keep trying to mix up the powder at the bottom that never completely dissolves. Even if you stirred it for hours in a gallon of hot water.

But part of her almost wishes she was there doing exactly that. No, it wasn't because her sons were playing. She had been hearing noises around the house lately. And outside around the yard. It's true her paranoia had been in overdrive ever since splitting with her first husband. She hadn't heard from him in quite a while, but that didn't mean she was done with him. Even the restraining order she got before they were divorced didn't stop him. In fact, it only seemed to further enrage him. It was only after the cops arrested him for the second time that he started to get the hint and move on with the rest of his life. She was so relieved when the late-night visits and phone calls stopped, but she always had the feeling he was still watching her.

She still wonders what she ever saw in him. How she fell for the phony charm of a smooth-talking salesman. She still kicks herself for not being able to see it right from the first time they met. It would have saved her so much heartache. How she managed to live under the same roof with him for two and a half years was nothing short of miraculous. There was all the drinking. The drugs. The erratic behavior. Even though she was devastated when she had the miscarriage, it turned out to be such a blessing in disguise. The mere thought of bearing his child still makes her nauseous.

Yet this weekend seemed different somehow. She was convinced it wasn't just her imagination. But she looked outside all around the house and found nothing out of the ordinary. The tracks were probably just from the squirrels. Lord knows there were enough of them. Especially being in a heavily wooded area along the river where they were. Or maybe it was a raccoon or a possum. Aaron said he saw a muskrat last summer. Maybe that was it. Or even a beaver. They've been known to be around as well.

But there was more than just noises around the house.

There was a lot more activity than normal on the street. Cars driving really slow past the house. Not just the usual gawkers who were acting as if they had never seen a big house before. Heck, theirs wasn't even all that nice. There were much nicer ones a few doors away. And a whole lot bigger. The older exterior of their house was charming. It had character. That she had to admit. Because without it, there was no way she would ever have settled for something so tiny. Even then, there were times she regretted it. With only 2,300 square feet, sometimes it felt like they were tripping over each other. And it didn't even have a pool. All they had was a hot tub out back with a view of the river. But it was such a great deal, Aaron said. Less than a million. Just think what a great investment it will be! And we don't have to max out our line of credit. Whatever. The truth was that their neighbors had so much more. Pools. Saunas. Cathedral ceilings. Marble floors. Circular driveways. Bigger lots. There are times she's so embarrassed she feels like putting a bag over her head whenever she hosts a dinner party.

Then there were the people hanging around. Not just the usual joggers in packs of five or six going by, forcing cars to get out of their way. But the rabble. Workmen. It was especially odd given that it was on a weekend. Most just work Monday to Friday unless there's an emergency. There was a Shaw Cable van parked up the street for almost the whole day on Saturday and well into the evening. Even if he was doing an installation, it wouldn't take *that* long. And the guy hardly ever got out of his van. Not that she could blame him in this weather. Maybe he was just milking overtime. Tradesmen will do anything to pad their bill. And yet they insist on sticking to the letter of their contract. Painters are especially bad that way. When she asked the guy who did their garage to do the shed as well, he said it would be an extra charge. *The bloody gall!*

But what really creeped her out was the guy she saw early Saturday morning. While sipping on a latte by the big picture window overlooking the back yard, she saw a white van pull into the parking lot at the community club across the river. She didn't pay much attention to it at first. She expected a bunch of kids to pile out the side door or out the back with their hockey gear. There were always games going on there. But no one got out. It just sat there at the edge of the lot closest to their house. So she got up to get the binoculars. And when she went right up to the window to look outside, it suddenly took off. Maybe it was a coincidence, she thought. With her dinner party that night, she forgot about it until Sunday afternoon, when she saw the same van parked in the same spot where it was on Saturday morning. Perhaps it was a city maintenance truck, she thought. But when she got the binoculars, this time she saw a guy at the edge of the riverbank with a tripod and a camera with a long lens aimed in their direction.

So she jumped in the Beemer. Told Aaron she needed to pick something up at the store. She said she would only be a few minutes. She didn't want to tell him the real reason, especially when it would probably amount to nothing. Just like all the other times she thought she was being watched. Still, she had to be sure. She would go bananas otherwise. But when she got there, the van had gone. The van's tracks were there, sure enough. Looked like he peeled out pretty quickly. She even saw the spot in the snow where he had set up his tripod. It left her with more questions than answers. Was her paranoia running wild again? Was she ready to be committed?

She tries to put it behind her as she turns away from the window and looks up at the valance, where she notices another couple of dust bunnies. She will be sure to mention it when she talks to Priscilla tomorrow. She feels sorry for Priscilla with her special-needs child and all. But she can't keep leaving dust bunnies around like that and still expect to have a job. She did a pretty lousy job of cleaning up after Saturday night's dinner party too. Leah sure never had to raise hell like that with Ramona, her last maid. Ramona would never leave the house that way. She was really good. Leah pleaded with her to stay. "I am so sorry, Mrs. Leah," she said. It was always Mrs. Leah. Just like Priscilla calls her. Never Mrs. Berkowitz-Klein. "I have to go home. My mother is sick. I am needed to take care of her." But why her, Leah asked. Couldn't one of her siblings have tended to her dying mother? Surely there were plenty to choose from. They multiply like rabbits in those Asian countries. One of Aaron's patients once said half-jokingly that the gestation period for a Filipino woman must be only six weeks. And even without any other family, surely they could just put her in a nursing home the way everyone else does. Why did Ramona have to go all the way back to the Philippines? Leah offered her a little raise to get her to change her mind, but she wouldn't budge.

Her cappuccino is still warm as she takes another sip on her way to the sofa, where she decides that once she's finished, she will use the time while Aaron and the kids are gone to soak in the Jacuzzi. It would do her a world of good. In addition to everything at home, things have been nonstop at work lately. A new production is coming this weekend and it was already the talk of the town. It got front-page coverage in the Arts & Life section of the paper and had been all over the radio and TV. The first few performances had been sold out for a month and there were only scattered singles left for the rest. After she had seen the show on Broadway, it instantly became one of her favorites. Needless to say, it was quite a coup to be able to bring it to Winnipeg. They were even able to get one of the original lead actors to perform. He was absolutely wonderful when she saw him in person. He had such a beautiful singing voice. She'd love to see him perform in the opera.

Then suddenly it goes dark.

It's the power. It's gone out. Again. *Damn it!* For all the hydroelectric power the province produces and exports, Manitoba Hydro can't provide stable power to their own people when they need it the most. Like now, in the middle of another Arctic deep freeze. Sometimes she feels like they're living in some third-world country. It's at times like this she wishes she had listened to Aaron. Ever the pragmatist. Let's get a portable generator, he said after their power was out for more than a day last February. *It's not like it hasn't happened before. We need to be prepared for the next time it happens.* But they'll fix the problem this time, she said. Except that it keeps going out. Again and again. It's not so bad in the summer. Even if the house turns into an oven, at least the pipes aren't going to freeze. So much for that relaxing soak in the Jacuzzi. Now she'll have to dig out her mink coat and bundle up. If the power doesn't come back soon, she'll have to build a fire. And listen to Aaron gloat when he gets home. *See, I told you it was going to happen.*

But before she can bundle up and wait out the latest outage, she has to find her phone so she can call Hydro. And be put on hold for an hour to try to get through to some recent immigrant from Somalia who drew the short straw in getting the night shift to report the outage and try to find out when the power is coming back on. But after getting up, she notices the streetlights are still on. And she sees the reflection from the lights in the neighbor's window next door. *They're hot, why aren't we? Usually when the power goes out, the whole neighborhood gets hit.*

After putting down her cup, she treads carefully through the darkness with her hands out to her side like a blind man who lost his white cane, hoping she'll be able to find the phone. *Did I leave it in the living room? Or in the bedroom? No, it's probably in the living room.* Making her way past the staircase directly opposite the front door into the living room, she also wishes she could find a flashlight. She knows they have one. They used it the last time the power went out. But instead, she bumps into a table. Then she hears a crash. Something smashed to bits. Probably that lovely vase. *Damn!* The vase she paid an arm and a leg for in that boutique in Milan. Feeling her way with both hands along the wall on her right, she moves on. One baby step at a time. She sure doesn't want to bump into anything else. Slowly passing through an entranceway, she feels the door handles of the fridge. *At least I know where I am!* Moving on past the counter, she feels the phone on the wall. *Oh yeah, we've got a landline too. That'll work!*

She picks up the receiver and puts it to her ear.

The line is dead.

Oh God!

Chapter 3

Luck of the Damned
Monday, January 15, 6:49 PM

Mitch couldn't believe his good fortune. *Luck of the damned!*

He was just getting ready to pack up for the night and head home when he saw the Escalade back out of the driveway. Without Leah in the front passenger's seat. *What gives? Doesn't she want to see her own kids play? Her own flesh and blood? Or does she have other plans? Must be something pretty important if she does.* He figured for sure the two of them would be going. Each of the two kids had a game that night. Caleb and David. The kids he should have had with her. One of which was slaughtered while it slept in the womb. She called it a miscarriage, of course. She even paid off the doctor to lie for her. So sorry, the doctor said. There was nothing they could do. A terrible tragedy. But he knows the truth. She had an abortion. She couldn't bear the thought of bearing his child. He only wishes he could prove it.

He checked with the community club earlier in the day and confirmed the kids' games. They even published the rosters. Caleb would be playing in the indoor rink, while David was in outdoor rink #2. Caleb plays right wing and is the team's leading goal scorer. Figures. He's a real show-off too. Wonder where he got it from. David is a defenseman and leads his team in assists. At the couple of games Mitch saw him play, the kid showed some real puck-handling skills. He might have a future in hockey if he sticks with it.

At first, Mitch didn't trust his eyes. And with the stakes being so high, he couldn't afford to make a mistake. So he pulled out his night vision binoculars. Not only was the passenger's seat empty, but she was in the window waving good bye to them. More importantly, she was dressed in something casual. At least by her standards. Nothing she would want to be seen out in public in. If she was going somewhere, she'd be dressed to the hilt. Like the real fashionista she is. No, she didn't have other plans. She was staying home. Probably sitting by the fire curled up with a good book. Giving him a priceless opportunity to make his move. One he couldn't afford to waste. Especially since she's onto him. As he figured she would be. He's seen her looking back at him with the binoculars. She even got in the car and came after him yesterday. She's obviously on high alert since she's got to know Mitch isn't long for this world. No doubt, Dr. Hussain tipped her off even before giving him the news. That's probably why she was whooping it up at her dinner party on Saturday night. Celebrating his impending death. But he'd see to it she wouldn't be doing much more celebrating. One way or another.

Over the weekend, he had been bandying about a number of plans as to how he would handle it if such a golden opportunity didn't fall into his lap. The most obvious would be to just walk into her office and shoot her or bludgeon her to death. But there would be too many complications. He would only use that as a last resort. It would be much better if he could do it at her home. Since Klein and the kids were always around, he'd have to include them as well. He couldn't leave witnesses. He'd rather not have to bother with them, but Mitch certainly wouldn't feel sorry for Klein. He's been profiting from Leah's treachery, and anyone who cavorts with that floozy deserves their fate. As for the kids, he'd probably be doing the world a favor by removing the last of her children from the gene pool. Ideally, he'd subdue them all, put them in one of the cars in the garage, then start it and have them die of carbon monoxide poisoning. Make it look like a suicide. Like a mini-Jonestown. But if they put up a struggle, he was certainly up to the task of using the brute-force approach. He would make the whole thing look like a home invasion. Take a bunch of valuables on the way out to throw off the cops.

But thanks to this gift from God, he wouldn't have to worry about the rest of them. It would be just her and Mitch. Alone once again.

A few minutes after the Escalade disappeared from view, he backed up the truck and parked it down the street behind some trees where she couldn't see it. Then he made his way over the tall, black wrought-iron fence and into the yard. Cutting himself on the pointy finials that she probably sharpened herself. No doubt she also smeared them with her own piss and shit so he would get an infection. She deserves to die just for that alone. Then he nearly broke his arm when he fell over on the other side. Would have for sure if all the snow hadn't been there to help break his fall. There was no reason the damned bitch had to build her fence so high. It should be illegal to have such a high fence. Once he got back on his feet, he made his way through the deep snow to the back of the house.

After catching his breath, getting inside took him a bit of time, but he eventually picked the deadbolt lock on the back door. This was the one time he could not afford to use the Rambo approach. She would definitely have heard him if he had used a crowbar or broken a window and would have called the cops. For her, they would drop everything and send the cavalry with sirens blaring. Especially once they found out he was the suspect. Even though the back yard was covered in complete darkness, he also had to make sure to stay still and out of sight while picking the lock since the back door was right next to the big picture window. Otherwise, she'd surely see the shadows.

Once inside, he had to silently slip off his boots. Being wet, they'd squeak on the hardwood floors and would make quite the clumping sound. For this, he needed to be in stocking feet. And as he made his way down the stairs to the basement where the breaker panel and phone connection were, he knew that all the surveillance he had done over the years on Leah and the house was finally paying off. He still remembered the day he posed as a city worker checking the sewer system. The Filipino maid let him in without even checking the phony ID he had. Just told him to do what he needed and close the door on his way out while she went back upstairs to finish vacuuming. *It's amazing what a pair of white overalls and a rented white cargo van can get you.* With the hidden camera, he filmed every inch of the main floor and basement so he would be able to study the layout of the house in more detail at home. Which he did again this weekend just to refresh his memory.

Putting on his night vision goggles, he tiptoed down the stairs and found the breaker panel easily enough. Just where he remembered it. Flipping off the power was simple, but cutting the phone line was a little trickier. The wires were so bloody tiny. And he had to carefully study the cabling panel before pulling anything out. He needed to be sure to leave everything just like he found it.

Back upstairs, he slid his way along the wall toward the living room, where he got another stroke of good fortune when he found Leah's cell phone on the table by the window. He grabbed it right away, then turned it off and stuffed it in his pocket. *No one's coming to save you now, you bitch!* Then he made his move when he heard her pick up the phone in the kitchen. For sure, she'd know something was up when she discovered the line was dead. She's an evil whore. One of God's worst creations. But she's not stupid. So he wasted no time in reaching around behind her and putting her in a choke hold until she was unconscious.

As he expected, Leah put up a hell of a fight. She scratched and clawed. Even drew a little blood. Made him have to do a little cleanup on the wall. She wanted to live, he had to give her that much. And she knew it was him. But in a New York minute, her favorite whipping boy had become her worst nightmare. There was nothing she could do. When she finally fell to the ground, she was now his once again. And she will stay his.

He thought about finishing the job right then and there. *Oh, was it tempting!* But he didn't want to kill her quite yet. She had to be made to suffer first. Just like she had made him suffer ever since the two had first met. He had a score to settle. He knew he couldn't hope to get even. It was impossible. But he had to at least tip the scales a little more in his favor before meeting his maker. So instead, he just injected her with enough ketamine to keep her out for a while. Then he tied her up and bagged her for the trip north.

Where he will teach her a lesson.

Her final lesson.

Chapter 4

Waking Up
Tuesday, January 16, 6:51 AM

Leah wakes up.

She feels groggy. In a fog. As if she's been out for a hundred years. Like Rip Van Winkle. *What the hell happened?* As she slowly regains her senses, she realizes something is terribly wrong. It is dark. She can see nothing. She has no idea where she is, but she knows she's not at home. That much she's sure of. She feels a blindfold tied so snugly around her head that it's pressing on her eyes. She begins to feel cold. Not just cold because she has been stripped completely naked save for the blindfold, but because it's cold. Damn cold. She instinctively wants to wrap her arms around her shivering body, but they are tied behind her back. She is lying flat on her back on a blanket so thin and full of holes she can feel the chilly concrete beneath it. She wants to sit up, but when she jerks her head up, the metal collar strapped around her neck nearly chokes her. After coughing a couple of times, she tastes the blood in her mouth and feels something puffy inside. She begins to feel the dull pain in her cheekbones. Then she rubs her tongue around and feels the sharp edges of several broken teeth. *Boy, is Aaron going to have a big job fixing this!*

Her attention returns to the frigid air. It consumes her above all her other aches and pains. Until she begins to feel the throbbing pain between her legs. She realizes that in addition to being beaten, she has probably been raped. *Oh, dear God! Wasn't beating me up good enough?* She wants to cry. Curl up in bed and pull the covers over her head and stay there for a month. The thought of what has happened to her is just too much to bear. The tears begin flowing and quickly saturate the blindfold. Not that it helps. She remembers what happened to Sheila. Her colleague was going out to her car on her way home. The way she always did. Except this time, three big Indians followed her into the garage. Just before she got to her car, they grabbed her and dragged her away. The surveillance video showed she put up quite a struggle. But it didn't do her any good. When they got her into the stairwell, they beat the shit out of her and gang-raped her. Physically, she recovered. But she became a different person. Split with Mark. Even lost custody of the kids. Then she lost her job. The director was sympathetic, of course. But there was only so much he could take. She wasn't showing up half the time. When she did show up, she would blow up at the smallest things. Everyone was walking on eggshells around her. The final straw was when she yelled at the CEO of one of their major sponsors. They had no choice but to let her go. Then a couple of months later, she drove her car off a bridge into the Red River and drowned. The autopsy showed her system was full of alcohol and drugs. It was such a tragedy. Police eventually found those Indians. But after the trial, the judge let them off. Blamed it on their bad upbringing. As if that justified what they did to her. It's still difficult for Leah to think about even after all this time.

She just wants to go home. Try to forget this ever happened. But first, she has to get out of here. Wherever *here* is. Given how cold it is, she might be in a freezer or refrigerator. But then a musty smell begins to invade her nostrils. She thinks she might be in someone's basement. In a house where the heat's been turned off. She wonders if anyone even knows she's there. So she tries to scream for help, but her voice crackles. She can barely get out more than a screech. Her throat is sore. And her mouth is dry.

She hears someone angrily grabbing a door handle. It is instantly followed by the sound of a door slamming on the side of a wall and the pitter-patter of rubber-soled shoes scampering down a few wooden stairs.

Then she feels his breath. Smells it.

Even before he pulls the blindfold off, she knows she was right.

It's *him*.

Chapter 5

Face to Face

Tuesday, January 16, 6:54 AM

After tossing the blindfold aside, Mitch stares at the butt-ugly creature in front of him chained up like a dog to the pole in the middle of the crawl space, barely lit by the 30-watt bulb near the stairs. All wrinkled. Droopy boobs. *She sure let herself go. Looks a lot different now without those designer clothes on. She's put on way too much weight. If it wasn't for the kids, for sure Klein would have left her by now.* And so full of hate. Such anger in those eyes. To think this was the woman he once loved and wanted to spend the rest of his life with. To have her as the mother of his children. Now he can barely stand the sight of her. He still can't believe how he let himself be lured into her trap. He should have seen it right away, even while they were dating. But he got sucked in. And boy did she make him suffer. God, how she made him suffer. Belittled him. Treated him like shit. All after he had worked so hard to give her everything she wanted. Then in the end, all he got in return was betrayal. For this, she must pay. And she will.

That betrayal consumed him. Not just when he was at the house, but ever since they split up. Much as he tried to forgive her, he never really got over it. What really puzzled him was why she would do him over like that. Be so vindictive. So cruel. His mother taught him that there was goodness in every person, but try as he did, he could never find it in Leah. Some people are just plain evil. He found that out the hard way. But despite all she had done to him, he had not let himself be distracted the night before at her house. He needed a clear head. First and foremost, he had to hook up the phone wires again. That was a bitch. Even with the punch down tool he stuck in his pocket. Then, after turning the power back on, he had to make sure to wipe down anything he had touched with his bare hands. His fingerprints are on file. They'd connect the dots in an instant if they got the bright idea of dusting the place. The keys to her silver Mercedes were easy enough to find. She left them hanging on a hook in the kitchen. But finding her purse took some time. She probably deliberately hid it away, knowing he might be coming. But that didn't stop him. He had to find it. And he did. Eventually. Hopefully he hadn't made too much of a mess in her bedroom. He tried to put things back as best he could. But that was a wild card he hadn't prepared for.

He was surprised that the Mercedes wasn't very roomy. He thought for sure he'd be able to lay her flat. Instead, he had to scrunch her up in the fetal position. If only Klein hadn't taken the Escalade. It would have been perfect. He thought about using the van, but he needed one of her cars to make it look like she just flew the coop. It was why he also took her purse. Good thing he did too since he didn't have that much cash on him and the bitch left the tank almost empty. Probably drained it deliberately to try to foil him. So he dug inside and found her wallet. Thankfully, she had some cash. Not a lot, but enough so he could fill up the tank. She probably had a lot more around the house somewhere. Maybe under the mattress. Or in her closet. Not just to hide it from him, but also from Klein. For all Mitch knew, she might have been planning to run out on Klein like she ran out on him. But he didn't have time to hunt around for it. It was a shame, because Klein and the kids didn't need it. He was well off. And she sure wouldn't be needing it anymore. Where she was going, she needed to travel light.

He was finally able to relax a little when he got on the highway for the hour-long drive north. There wasn't a soul in sight. And he made sure no one could find him because of that device he brought to jam the GPS tracker she had in the Mercedes. You can never be too prepared, so it seems. All he had to do was plug it into the lighter. Just to be on the safe side, however, he made sure to strip the tracker out and rip out the battery before taking off.

It had been a while since he had driven a car with as much pep as her Mercedes. Ever since Leah cleaned him out in the divorce, he couldn't afford anything nicer than the Camaro. Then he had to settle for the Journey after getting screwed over in the accident. *God, what a piece of shit!* So he had to make an extra effort to keep the Mercedes just under the speed limit. Just in case there was an eager Mountie who happened to be out past his bedtime. Besides, the highway was covered in ice, and he sure didn't need to get into another accident. They had obviously plowed it since the most recent storm. The Interlake got hit even worse than they did in Winnipeg. But as usual, they didn't plow down to the pavement, leaving a nice little layer of ice behind. *Should have left it bloody well alone. At least you can get some traction on the snow and won't spin around like a top and end up in the ditch.*

When he reached his destination, he wasn't surprised that the town hadn't gotten around to plowing the streets around the house. They probably hadn't done it after the last storm either. For all he knew, they might not have been around all winter. Couldn't really blame them. Only ones around town at this time of year are the ice fishers, and they're out by the marina. But as luck would have it, a few snowmobilers had come through recently and he was able to follow their tracks up to the driveway. That's where he really ran into trouble. He had to get out and shovel just to get to the garage door. Bloody snow was frozen hard as a rock. It took him long enough, but he eventually got the Mercedes inside. Where no one will find it for months.

He then dragged Leah out of the back seat and retied her hands behind her back before hurling her down the steps into the crawl space while he figured out what to do with her. He took off his parka in the living room, and as he wiped all the snow off his pants, he saw Rex's collar hanging on a hook by the front door. Grandpa's old rottweiler. Mitch had forgotten about Rex. Rex was an awful dog. Chased everything that moved. Growled at everyone. But Grandpa loved him and he was heartbroken when the big fleabag keeled over. Kept Rex's old collar as a keepsake. And that old collar was perfect for the occasion.

His first thought was to tie her to the post on the bed in the guest room. But that would be too good for her. Not to mention that it would be a shame to ruin some perfectly good bedsheets. Let her spend her final hours in a tiny crawl space shivering on a concrete floor instead. A fitting demise for someone who had led such a wretched existence here on Earth. Hell will be too good for her.

Stripping her naked brought back all the rage that had been building for so long, even while they were still married. So he balled up his fist and hit her smack-dab in the middle of the face. He couldn't help himself. And he kept hitting her. Harder and harder each time. It felt so good. It was the best form of cathartic release he could have imagined. Better than any drug. The feeling was incredible. Here he was, finally with the upper hand over the woman who had so cruelly tormented him. And she deserved every bit of it. Even if he did get a little carried away. Broke her nose. Heard other bones crack too. And some teeth. For the final bit of punishment though, he wanted to have her awake. He wanted her to feel it. To look into his eyes as he was having his way with her for one last time. So before slipping his pants down, he grabbed her by the neck. Shook her like a rag doll. But she wouldn't wake up. Just kept moaning and passing out. Even after smacking her across the face a few more times. That bit of pleasure she had to deny him. So he just threw her back down, spread her legs and did her right there. Quick. Surgically efficient. When he was done, looking down at her prone, naked body while pulling up his pants, he was finally satisfied that he had been able to exact some small measure of revenge. If he had done it a million times over, it still wouldn't come close to evening up the score, but he had at least tilted the playing field back in his favor a little. *You never did deserve the honor of being Mrs. Mitch Schubert, you little bitch! I'm glad you kept using Berkowitz. You deserve to die here. Naked and alone.*

"Mitch?" Leah asks in a faint, screechy voice.

"As if you needed to ask."

"Wh . . . why?"

"*Why?*" Mitch asks incredulously as he snaps his head back and hits the back of it on a joist, giving him a quick reminder that there is only about three feet of headroom in the crawl space.

"*Why?*" he repeats as he rubs the back of his head, angry at himself for forgetting about the low clearance, but more angry at Leah for making him do it. Then he doubles up his fist and pile-drives it squarely into her already bloodied face.

"You dare ask *why*? After all you've done to me . . ."

Bobbing her head to the right, Leah whines weakly as Mitch continues.

"Shut up, you miserable bitch!" he yells as he again rubs the back of his aching skull with his right hand. As Leah keeps moaning, using his free left hand, he slaps her face back and forth a few times. The blood and groaning spur him on to swat her faster and faster and more violently each time. Only when he tires himself out does he stop and return his focus to the throbbing pain in the back of his head.

A half-minute later, still visibly woozy and with blood still trickling down from her cheeks, Leah musters up the energy to address her captor once again.

"Wh . . . what . . . what do you want?"

Mitch isn't paying attention. Slumped on his side, leaning on the back wall with his right hand on the back of his head, he's still preoccupied with the razor-sharp pain at the spot where he hit it.

"Is this about money?" Leah asks. "Is it money you're looking for?"

Mitch picks his head up.

"You mean your ill-begotten fortune? You must be worth a few mill by now. Probably got a big stash in a Swiss bank account you're hiding from Klein. But no, that's not what I'm looking for. Maybe at one time. But not now. It's a little late for that."

Mitch gets on all fours and crawls over and past Leah toward the door, being careful to keep his head down, then slowly rises to an upright position as he climbs the stairs. Back up on the ground floor, he heads over to the door to the attached garage and spots the ax he had left standing upside down leaning against the wall. He grabs the handle with one hand, but it's heavy. He needs two hands. So with both hands on it, he slowly drags the ax down to the basement, one step at a time, banging it on the stairs as he goes.

He again pays his captive no attention as she shrieks at the sight of the ax. He crouches down on both knees, moves up on her right near her midsection before laying the ax down. Then he turns to face her, looking her squarely in the eyes. Eyes that are now filled with fright. She knows her time on Earth is only seconds away from coming to an end. *Karma's a bitch, ain't it, dear?*

He reaches out with his left hand and gently strokes her face, puffy, swollen and covered with blood. Some of it's fresh. Some old. She winces as his index finger goes over the bridge of her broken nose. But when his pinky strays between her lips, she opens her mouth and bites it. He yelps as he jerks his hand back and grabs it with his right. Only after a few seconds does he take his right hand away to look at the wound. He glances back at her and notices the fragments of teeth she cut him with still dripping with droplets of his blood. *Such hostility, Mrs. Klein!*

With that, he grabs the handle of the ax with both hands and presses the toe right up against her Adam's apple, just above the dog collar around her neck. "That's the last thing you're ever going to do to me. Because now you're going to get yours," he says with a big shit-eating grin on his face.

"Stop it, Mitch! Don't do it!" she yells as he continues to press the ax against her throat, puncturing the skin and drawing a trickle of blood. "Spare me. Please!"

Mitch's jaw drops.

"Spare you?" he asks. "Spare you? Why should I spare you? You're a despicable human being who has more than earned a ride on an express elevator to hell. And I'm here to get that ride started. Right now."

"Think of my children. They need their mother. They've done nothing to you."

"You think I'm going to worry about any child of yours? Come to think of it, I might actually be doing them a favor. Maybe Klein will show some better judgment the next time around and take up with someone a little less trashy than you. Someone who might instill them with better values. Give them a fighting chance to be decent people. Not to be parasites like their mother is. Or *was.*"

Leah screams as Mitch slowly presses the ax deeper into her neck. He doesn't just want to chop her head off. That would be quick and painless. That she doesn't deserve. No, he wants her to suffer as she slowly bleeds to death. And he wants to watch every second of it. To watch his ingenious plan that came together perfectly pay off. His eyes get wide as saucers as the trickle of blood turns into a swift-flowing creek. Leah keeps screaming as he pushes the ax still deeper, puncturing her trachea, so Mitch takes his right hand off the ax and tightly cups it over Leah's mouth to muffle the sound. He wants nothing to distract from this special moment. *God, why didn't I do this years ago? Before she married Klein and got pregnant. Stop her from spreading her germ seed.*

He is suddenly overcome by a piercing headache. It is not at the spot where he hit his head on the joist. It is deep inside his skull. Where the cancer is eating away at his brain. The cancer that he knows will kill him. His hands begin to tremble. Then his entire body. He can do nothing to stop it. It is like he stuck his finger in a socket and can't pull it out. Still with the ax in his grasp, he falls on his side, hitting his head on the concrete floor.

Then it goes dark.

Chapter 6

The Detective
Tuesday, January 16, 7:44 PM

Treading carefully in her high heels, detective Sierra Kowalski inches her way down the long, dark driveway of the Wellington Crescent estate belonging to Dr. Aaron Klein and his wife, Leah Berkowitz-Klein, nearly slipping and falling on the ice and snow. *For all the dough these rich Jews around here rake in, surely they can get someone to plow the goddamned driveway. Didn't figure I'd have to wear my boots!*

It was less than an hour ago that she got the call. Just as she was ready to step into the shower following another row with Victoria. Getting calls like these at all hours of the day and night made her wish she had never applied for the open detective position in the Homicide Unit. At least when she was walking the beat on the graveyard shift after graduating from the Academy, she had regular hours. Not that she didn't try to get a day shift. Filed a grievance over it. She was, after all, a member of a disadvantaged and underrepresented target group. The union lawyer said that made it a *prima facie* case for discrimination. But even though the committee was sympathetic, they didn't rule in her favor. She needed more seniority. Try again in a year, they said. In this case, however, the call from her boss was welcome. It was damned cold outside, par for the course at this time of year in Manitoba, but not as frosty as things had become at home.

It certainly wasn't like that at the beginning after the two of them had first met at Switch Hitters, Winnipeg's hottest gay and lesbian club. Sierra had just been accepted into the Winnipeg Police Service after finishing her undergraduate program at the University of Winnipeg, where she was majoring in women's and gender studies with a minor in criminal justice. And Victoria was just getting started with her career as the late-night weather girl. With her drop-dead gorgeous looks, long, flowing blond hair, double Ds and camera presence, they scooped her up right after she graduated. It was love at first sight for Sierra, and the two of them hit it off right away. She normally doesn't sleep with someone on the first date, but this was one time she just couldn't help herself. It was true that they were both plastered and had been doing coke, but she would have jumped in the sack with her even before doing her first line.

It was a whirlwind romance and it wasn't long before they bought a condo to begin their life together. They had even begun planning their wedding. They hadn't set a date, but they'd been shooting for the fall. October or early November. They were going to have a big service with all the trimmings, with a guest list that could fill that big, majestic cathedral across from Central Park. Right in the heart of the city. It would be the social event of the year. Then, for their honeymoon, they would jet off to the Bahamas. Spend a couple of weeks frolicking on the beach at a private resort. They even put down a deposit to secure their spot. It was like she was living a dream.

But November had come and gone. And neither of them had brought up the subject again. Sierra wasn't even sure if they were officially engaged anymore. Lately, Sierra had been sleeping more and more on the pull-out sofa in the living room. She didn't want to disturb Victoria, she said. But both of them knew the real reason. They had become little more than roommates who had had just about enough of each other. It seemed like it was just a matter of time before one of them moved out. Probably the only thing holding them back at this point was that neither of them could find the time in their hectic work schedules to find a new place.

Even before all the wedding talk and the formal engagement, however, they had been slowly drifting apart as their respective careers began to take off. Especially for Victoria. From humble beginnings, she had become the city's favorite spokesmodel. The attention-grabbing picture of her in that low-cut, long black sequin gown she did for the car dealership was all over town. Billboards, bus shelters, you name it. Everywhere they went, people would stop her on the street and say, "You got it, Fairway Ford!" Just like it said in the ad. And Victoria loved it. Every bit of it. Not that Sierra begrudged her for all the notoriety she was getting. But it had made Victoria a different person. She had gotten way too big for her britches. As Sierra's uncle would say, they don't make headgear big enough for her anymore. The once kind, considerate and down-to-earth girl Sierra fell in love with at first sight had become totally self-absorbed. The obscure Victoria Cirelli had become Vickie C, the big media celebrity. Or maybe she had always been that way and Sierra just chose to look the other way. It's possible. Love is blind, as they say.

And though she would never admit it to Victoria, Sierra was just as guilty of letting her own career get in the way of their relationship. There sure hadn't been much time for the two of them ever since she was accepted into Homicide. It was a major step up the ladder professionally, not to mention the bigger paycheck, but it put her personal life in the toilet. When she first got the job, she wondered why

Norm, one of her new colleagues, said, "Be careful what you wish for, kid." But she soon found out what he meant. Maybe, with some work on both of their parts, the relationship was still salvageable. But it had reached a point where Sierra didn't care enough to salvage it. Heck, Sierra didn't even *like* Victoria anymore. And there was the fact that she didn't find Victoria all that attractive anymore either. Or any other woman for that matter. All the way through high school and into university, she thought being with a woman was so cool. And it made her somebody. Part of the "in" crowd. Especially for gold star lesbians like her. They were special. It was the socially responsible thing to do, they said. Being straight was so passé. Something your grandparents did. But now she's not sure what to think anymore.

Whatever the case, there's no way she'd have gotten on the force at all, let alone been accepted into Homicide so soon without being a lez. Being so petite, she fell way short of the physical standards. And there was no way she could ever hope to pass the physical abilities test. She'd die before getting through one lap around the gym, let alone six. And forget about lifting 80 pounds. That just wasn't happening. She barely weighed 80 pounds. But they had employment equity quotas to fill in addition to a renewed effort to recruit and promote more dykes because of the high-profile scandal last year involving that lesbian homicide inspector who got a big payout after suing the Service. As they told Sierra in the interviews, anyone with homophobic tendencies, however small, is being rooted out right from top to bottom. Diversity and inclusion workshops are mandatory for all City employees now, and the Service is more proactive in ensuring gays and lesbians are given first dibs on all available positions and receive other benefits including a salary supplement to overcome systemic discrimination.

Using her right hand on the cruiser parked in front of the four-car garage to steady herself as she ambles her way toward the house, she catches sight of her old partner at the top of the stairs waiting for her, all bundled up and shivering. Just like she is.

"So Homicide got the call, eh?" asks Constable Darren Luke as she gets nearer to the house. It was a question Sierra herself asked after her phone rang. As her boss filled her in on the details, it sounded more like a case for the Missing Persons Unit, not Homicide. According to the husband, there were no signs of forced entry. Nothing around the house seemed abnormal aside from a little mess in the bedroom. The wife's purse was gone as was one of the cars. She seemingly just got in the car and split. Happens more often than people realize. But the husband insisted she wasn't like that. She just wouldn't run off. Certainly not without the children. She loved them. And him. He said they weren't having marital problems and she had no history of mental health issues. But ever since that high-profile case of the lady whose bones were recently discovered after she disappeared a couple of years ago, seemingly every missing person case gets shunted to Homicide now.

"Yeah, lucky me," Sierra says after scaling the icy concrete stairs. "Let's go inside." *Of all the black and whites on the street, why did it have to be you?*

"Just like old times. Except we're in a little better area of town this time."

Darren wasn't kidding. Right after they graduated from the same class in the Academy, the two of them worked patrol together in the North End for a few months. Harlem on steroids, he called it. But it wasn't *that* bad. Yeah, there were some issues. And Darren did save her ass a couple of times. That much she had to grudgingly admit. But then there were the times like that night on Selkirk Avenue. That Aboriginal man just wanted money. Eighty cents. There's no way he'd have put the knife to her throat if Darren hadn't pulled the John Wayne act the instant he saw the blade. He kept insisting he saved her life, but the guy was harmless. He was just looking for a cup of coffee. A few kind words would have been a lot more appropriate than a WWE-style takedown.

Thankfully, she gets along much better with Superintendent Andrea Saluk, her new boss. The two of them could chat for hours. Like Sierra, Andrea was also a new recruit with only three and a half years on the force. She got the promotion after the old superintendent was demoted as part of the scandal involving the inspector. Yet everyone seems to hate Andrea with a passion. No one will admit it, but the only possible reason is jealousy. All because a woman got the promotion instead of one of them. And they can't handle it. *Boo hoo!* Just because they've been around for, like, forever, doesn't mean they're deserving. And because Sierra is sitting up front and gets along so well with Andrea, they've started calling her the teacher's pet. Maybe if they made the effort to get to know Andrea the way she has, they wouldn't be so bitter.

Darren shows Sierra inside and the two of them stop in the foyer, where he pries off his heavy winter boots while she shakes off the dainty pink high-heeled shoes covering her ice-cold tootsies. Looking over at the row of boots, she is green with envy. *Would it be wrong to help myself to one pair on my way out? They might not even notice.*

"Has anyone else been here?" asks Sierra.

"Nope. I was the first one here. Spoke to the good doctor. Dentist, actually. He's acting like a real basket case. Can't say I blame him though."

Maybe not, she thinks as she glances to her left inside the study, where she spots a guy sporting a two-day-old growth in a white dress shirt getting up out of an easy chair and heading their way. Must be at least six-foot-two. *Fills out that Brooks Brothers shirt quite well. Probably spends a lot of time at the gym. Might even have a weight room around here. Certainly got the space for it.*

The pitter-patter of little feet suddenly interrupts her train of thought. Then she spots two excitable little kids out of the corner of her eye who come running up to her as if she were Santa Claus bearing a truckload of toys.

"I am sorry, madam," says a Filipino woman hurriedly running down the stairs behind them as Sierra gets down on her knees to greet the boys. *Probably the maid.*

"No problem," says Sierra, who keeps her focus on the bubbly youngsters. "So what are your names?" she asks.

"I'm Caleb," says the taller boy. "And this is my little brother, David."

"Pleased to meet you. I'm Sierra."

"Do you know where Mommy is?"

"Well, no, Caleb, I don't," she replies a bit hesitantly, taken aback by the direct question. "But we're going to find her. I promise. Soon. But I need to talk to your daddy first. OK?"

"OK."

"Good night, boys," she says as the maid gathers the kids and ushers them up the stairs and back to their rooms. *Rooms that are probably about three times bigger than mine.* Still smiling, Sierra gets back to her feet and turns to face the man she presumes is their father.

"Dr. Aaron Klein," he says as he extends his hand. She notices a nervous smile on his face and bags under his eyes. *Probably hasn't slept in the last 36 hours.* But as they taught her at the U of W, in cases like this, the husband is automatically the prime suspect and for good reason. Because he's the most likely person to have a motive. Could be something like an argument that got out of hand. One thing led to another and now she's dead. Then he put her body in a drum and dumped it in the river. Just like what happened not too long ago when they found that woman in a barrel in the basement of a rooming house. It was the boyfriend, of course. Did it in a jealous fit. Except that he didn't call the cops. Nonetheless, Sierra needs to keep an open mind and keep her suspicions to herself. The moment the doctor gets an inkling that he's a suspect, he'll lawyer up and go on the offensive. For all she knows, he's already got a high-powered lawyer friend looking out for him. This is the best time for her to get some answers. Or at least some clues.

"You've obviously met our children," he adds. "And that was Priscilla, our housekeeper. She's been staying with the kids today."

"Detective Sierra Kowalski. I'm with the Homicide Unit."

Dr. Klein returns a puzzled look.

"We're simply covering all the bases, Dr. Klein."

"No, it's not that. I mean, um, I was expecting, well, um . . ."

"A man?"

"No, it's not that. It's just, well, um . . . Will your boss be coming?"

In other words, like, where's the real detective?

"I assure you, Dr. Klein, I'm fully qualified." *And probably better than some of those fat asses counting down the days until their Rule of 80 kicks in. The golden rule. The magic number when their age plus years of service reaches 80 and they can collect their full pension. They've probably got it down to the hour.* "Now why don't we sit down and you can fill me in from the beginning. When you first noticed your wife was missing."

Dr. Klein shows her into the study where he offers her a seat and then begins his narrative as Darren retreats to the foyer. *Guess he's heard it before.* Apparently Dr. Klein took the boys out to their hockey games at the community club last night and when they came home, his wife was gone. Just gone. Along with the silver Mercedes. Her purse and phone were gone too. He tried calling over and over again but just got voice mail. The doors were locked. Most everything in the house looked normal. The time was flashing on the stove and on the microwave, but it was probably another power outage. Happens all the time. There were a few things scattered around their bedroom. Right by where she kept her purse. Lately, she's been making a habit of keeping it well hidden away. Ever since she noticed something missing. She suspected Priscilla, though she never accused her. *Hmm, maybe she was in a hurry to take off somewhere. Maybe she got a call. Have to check cell phone records. Or maybe that's where the two of them had an argument. Most logical place for it.*

While writing all the relevant details in her notepad along with scribbling down those thoughts, she asks, "You don't think she's just gone somewhere? Some family emergency?"

"No. Not without letting me know. She just doesn't take off on a whim. She's not like that."

She makes a note to check with all the local hospitals. And the airport. The train station too. The usual places. Don't have to worry about the bus station anymore since they shut down the intercity bus services. And put an APB out on the car. She'd get the details from him. Color, make, model, plate number. Not much else to go on right now. Besides the doctor himself, of course.

"Anyone you know of who might possibly want to do harm to her?" *Every detective has to ask this question. It's the law.*

"None who I can think of. There is her ex. Mitch Schubert. It was a messy divorce. He kept hassling her and she had to get a restraining order against him. He did seem like a bit of a weirdo, but she hasn't heard from him in years."

Someone to check into.

"Maybe there's someone at her work. She's the director of the Prairie Theater Company. Maybe there's some pissed-off actor out there who didn't get a part he wanted or a wannabe screenplay writer whose production didn't get accepted. Who knows?!" he exclaims, throwing up his hands in despair. "Maybe some wacko out there followed her home. The PTC is in a pretty seedy area of town and people have been mugged in that parking garage. One of her colleagues, Sheila, I think her name was. Don't know her last name. She's since passed away, anyway. She was beaten up and raped in that garage after work. For all I know, the same thing's happened to Leah."

Could be.

Sierra wants to ask if they've been having any marital problems, but she knows there's no way Dr. Klein would admit it even if the two of them were at each other's throats. She'd have to check with some family members first. Tactfully, of course. See if they know anything.

After writing up some more notes, Sierra asks, "OK if I take a look around the house before the identification unit arrives?"

"It's standard procedure," she interjects before he has a chance to answer. Sierra was actually surprised they weren't already there. When Andrea called, she said she had already dispatched them. She knew they'd be pissed about being called off-hours. They always are. It's not a part of the job Sierra enjoys either. But those brutes live for the chance to string their yellow tape and block off a wide radius around any potential crime scene and keep it there for most of the day. Disrupt as much traffic as possible. Just because they can.

"Sure. Be my guest."

As she slowly rises up out of the chair, she gazes around on either side of the fireplace. With her eyes scanning up and down for anything out of the ordinary, she tiptoes out of the study and turns to her left down a hallway, passing the staircase. She stops as her eyes are drawn to a framed family portrait on the table next to a big puffy purple chair. She wants to pick it up and look at it a little closer. But she can't. *This is a potential crime scene.* The techs will nag the shit out of her when they pick up her fingerprints. Instead, she crouches down and stares at it. All four of them are in it. Proud parents. From the expressions on their faces, the kids would rather have been somewhere else, but they're smiling because the photographer is probably waving some silly looking stuffed animal with one hand while pressing the shutter with the other. She just can't take her eyes off it. This is the human part of the job they don't teach you at the Academy. When a seemingly normal family living the dream suddenly has their world blown to pieces by a hand grenade. Whether it was something gruesome like Dr. Klein strangling his wife or breaking her neck during a heated argument or a sicko following her home from work and abducting her. Or something less dramatic like Mom having a midlife crisis and deciding to fly the coop. It still sucks. Especially for the kids. Kids Sierra was hoping to have someday. But not before getting a new partner first. Whether or not that partner will be female is still up in the air.

She gets up out of her crouch and moves through a pair of French doors into a large living room. Feeling her way through the eerie darkness, she bumps into the back of a loveseat facing a gigantic picture window overlooking the yard. Outside, a handful of lights illuminate the trees. Though she can't see beyond the trees, she presumes there is a beautiful river view. *That's why the rich and famous have homes like this on Wellington Crescent.* After digging out the flashlight from her purse, she shines it off to her right, where she spots a glass door next to the window that opens up to a deck. On the deck is a big rectangular bin with a tarp on it, covered with snow. Probably a hot tub, she thinks. But it would also be a good place to hide a body. Not that she thinks Dr. Klein, if he did indeed kill his wife, would be so stupid as to dump her there. Still, it's another place to check once the yellow tape squad arrives. Just to tick off all the boxes in the report.

Turning around, Sierra spots an archway leading to the kitchen. Where there's a light on. *God, this place is laid out like an obstacle course. Guess they never heard of open concept back in the days of the covered wagons when this house was built.* Through the archway, she turns to her right and steps through the galley-style kitchen. All the cabinets are bright white, as is the fridge. *Not stainless steel?* On the fridge are a few magnets holding up a couple of cute crayon drawings by the boys. The countertops are black granite or maybe quartz. There are a couple of cups lying around and another in the sink along with some dirty plates and a few pieces of cutlery. *The last remains of a light supper, perhaps. Surprised they can even think about eating at a time like this.* Across from the sink are the oven and microwave. They're also bright white. *Looks like a bloody hospital.* As she moves on, she notices a phone on the wall mounted at head height next to the archway that leads back to the foyer. *So they do have a landline. Not a given these days.* The phone is burgundy red. The one thing in the kitchen that doesn't match. And isn't hospital white.

As she walks through the archway with her eyes focused on the phone, Sierra trips on the long twisted and tangled handset cord and falls awkwardly on the metal flashing separating the kitchen tile from the hardwood floor in the foyer. Moaning and grabbing her aching legs, she notices a cut just below her knee. The blood is slowly seeping through the torn stocking. She reaches for her purse and pulls out a Kleenex to dab the tiny wound while Dr. Klein comes to ask if she's all right following the big ka-bang. Then she snaps a look back at the cord that caused her to fall. *Why the hell would they leave a 99-foot cord sticking out like that? Especially with kids running around. One of them could fall and kill themselves.*

Still smarting, she hears the front door opening. Looking up, she sees a bunch of guys tramping in and pounding their big heavy boots on the doormat. *Must be the yellow tape squad.* As Dr. Klein helps her get back to her feet, she glances back toward the cord. A cord she wishes she could grab and toss into a dumpster. But then her eyes are suddenly drawn to a shiny spot on the wall just above the baseboard next to where the cord is hanging. She slips away from him, gets back down on all fours and crawls up to get a closer look. Grabbing her flashlight once again, she shines the light right on it and stares at it for a while before giving a once-over around the surrounding area. She sees that the rest of the wall is grimy and dusty. Not to mention that there's a few brown spots scattered about. Probably from all the sand and grit outside. Brown sugar, as she's heard it described around town. There's probably more sand on the snow-covered Winnipeg streets at this time of year than on Miami Beach. *Maybe the kids left their boots around here.* She reaches out to feel the shiny spot. *It's been washed recently. But only that spot. If it was the maid, why wouldn't she do the whole wall? Unless something specific happened here. Right by the phone. But what?*

By any chance, were you trying to call someone, Leah?

Chapter 7

Taking Out the Trash
Tuesday, January 16, 10:31 PM

Mitch couldn't decide if devouring a Bernie's burger or watching Leah's remains being hauled away was more satisfying. It was the latter, of course, though he did love Bernie's burgers. It was an iconic Winnipeg chain and he had practically grown up on them. Whenever his parents asked where he wanted to go for his birthday, it was always Bernie's. They had locations all over the city, including the one he was parked outside of at the corner of Selkirk and Salter. Ground zero for drug deals, rapes, stabbings, shootings, muggings, you name it. Even the cops were scared of this area. Mitch's only saving grace on this night is that the criminal element doesn't like the cold any more than he does. Most of his visits had been at their River Heights location near where he grew up and still lives.

He was awfully famished. With all that had been going on over the past day or so, he hardly had a chance to eat. So he made an effort to get here before they closed at 10. Only after getting his order did he go outside to toss the garbage bags into their dumpster. And now they were in the truck and on their way to the Brady Road landfill site, where all of Winnipeg's garbage ended up. And that woman was the filthiest garbage the city had to offer. There could be no more fitting place for her to go. Except maybe being ground up into a sticky paste and flushed down a toilet, where it would eventually end up in the big sewage lagoon otherwise known as the Red River. He had thought about leaving the body intact somewhere so Klein and the kids could have a proper burial. Throughout his life, Mitch had prided himself on his compassion. But not after what happened at the house.

He had so desperately wanted to watch her die. After all she had put him through, he had earned that right. But even that much he was denied. Another cruel trick of the gods. It had to have been all the stress she put him through that caused the seizure. Dr. Hussain said this might happen and damned if the bloody quack wasn't right for the first time in his life. Mitch did everything he could to revive her after waking up in a pool of her blood. But it was too late. The ax was buried deep in her neck. So he had to do the next best thing. He pulled out the ax and began hacking her into little pieces. First came the ankles. Then he cut her legs at the knees and again just below the pelvis. Those bones were no match for him and the ax he'd made sure to sharpen beforehand. He then chopped off her ring finger before cutting off both hands. She sure wouldn't be needing those rings anymore. Her marriage to Klein was over. And Mitch could probably pawn them for a few hundred bucks. If only he could have gotten back the wedding and engagement rings he gave her. After they split up, he could never understand why she always refused to return them. Only years later did he find out the real reason when he found them at a consignment shop on Corydon only a few blocks from his condo. Once again, it was all about money. Bleeding every last quarter out of him. Just like it was with the divorce. In retrospect, he shouldn't have been surprised. She was the greediest person he had ever known. She'd have sold out her own kids for an extra buck or two. He moved on and cut her arms at the elbows, then at the shoulders. It took some effort, but he was able to crack her breastbone, splitting her torso in two. After he took off the collar, severing her head at the neck was the most satisfying moment of all. He couldn't help but grab her head by the hair and stare at her face. The face he had seen in so many nightmares. It was why he knew he couldn't part with it. The rest of her parts, he stuffed into garbage bags. Let the buzzards and rats peck away at it. If they would want any of her rotten flesh. But he must make room in his freezer for her head.

Having taken care of business, he bagged up her parts after doing his best to wring out as much of the blood as possible. Then he mopped up the crawl space as best he could. It didn't need to be a perfect job. He certainly didn't have to worry about detectives finding the place. He just wanted to get rid of the excess blood so it wouldn't stink too much. And, depending on how things played out, he might be having more guests there. He needed to be prepared. Wouldn't want them to freak out on him when they saw all the blood. Finally, before going to bed and catching some much-needed shut-eye, he needed to clean himself up. He was covered in her blood from head to toe and desperately needed to wash away every trace of her DNA. So he took a long, hot shower and got into some clean clothes.

When he finally got up late in the afternoon, he needed a ride to get back into the city. Sadly, using Leah's Mercedes, nice as it was, wasn't an option. He had to figure that Klein would have called the police by that time and that they'd probably put out an APB on it. But he knew it wasn't going to be a problem. There were plenty of other choices nearby. It was just a matter of which one would suit him best. The one he settled on was the older-model wine-colored Chevy Impala sitting in the Asmundsons' garage on Lake Street. He'd have liked a nicer ride. But it was built like a tank and wouldn't stick out like a Mercedes or a Porsche. And even in the auto-theft capital of North America, it wouldn't be a prime target to be stolen again. Which was probably why the Asmundsons didn't even bother to lock the side door to their garage. And why they left a spare key hanging up on a hook on the wall. After all, who'd want it? Besides, this is a tight-knit cottage community where everyone knows each other. And at this time of year, they were all away for the winter. Getting out of the deep freeze. Many of them went to Florida or the Caribbean, but the Asmundsons were in Arizona, as always. So not only was it a free ride, he'd have it for as long as he needed it. He'd be a resident of Rosh Pina Cemetery by the time they even realized their car was gone. His only problem was having to clear all that damned snow away from the doors. He must have spent a couple of hours shoveling. He even had to turn on the lights so he could see what he was doing. Then when he finally got the car out of the garage, he got stuck in the driveway. If only the Jonassons, who live next door, hadn't sold their snow blower last year. They didn't figure they'd need it anymore after buying a condo in Palm Springs.

With the leaky bags in the trunk, he wanted to drive past Leah's house when he got back into the city. Kind of like what they do with a funeral procession. And he was curious to see what the cops were up to. But he couldn't get anywhere nearby. They were out in full force. Only residents were being allowed past the checkpoint. They even had Academy Road blocked off, which was a hell of a long way from the house. Got caught in one mother of a traffic jam as everyone was scrambling to get down side streets and find another way to the bridge. Took forever to get out of the area. Not a moment too soon as well. One never knows with so many cops around. In retrospect, it was foolish of him to take such an unnecessary risk. But the cops were probably too busy laughing at all the chaos they had created. They live for stuff like that.

After pulling into Bernie's parking lot an hour or so later and getting his order, heaving those bags in the dumpster and now watching them being trucked away finally brought some degree of closure to that part of his life. Seeing her again up close only served to dredge up all the demons he had been suppressing for so many years. It was only when he was stuffing those bags in the trunk that he truly began to realize the depth of the anguish she had caused him. The mental abuse left scars so deep they could not possibly heal if he lived to be 100. No doctor could prove it, of course, but there could be no doubt that the tumor growing like a mushroom cloud inside his skull had her fingerprints all over it. That would be her parting gift to him.

It was why she had to be the first. Not just because of how she deserved the ultimate punishment more than most if not all of the others. But because she would have been on increasingly high alert once she learned of his fate, if she hadn't already found out from Dr. Hussain's office. She'd know he'd be coming for her. And every passing day that she lived would have made it all the tougher, if not impossible to get to her. It was a wonder she hadn't hired a security detail to follow her around and patrol the grounds at her house. It wasn't as if she didn't have the money for it. Mitch doesn't even want to think of how much he had been forced to cough up as part of the divorce, not to mention all that Klein was worth. Plus she was raking in some pretty good coin herself. Now that the final chapter in the wretched life of Leah Berkowitz has been written, it would be safe to say that would go down as her greatest mistake. And her last.

But as gratifying as it is to watch her being hauled away in pieces in the back of a garbage truck, he cannot afford to spend another second basking in the glory of having rid the world of one of its most vile creatures. Mitch needs to put her far out of his mind. His time is short and he cannot afford to be distracted. Because he has so much more left to do.

Including taking out the piece of shit that's next on his list.

Chapter 8

A Long Day
Wednesday, January 17, 5:46 PM

Sierra desperately needs to get home, crawl under the covers and stay there for a month. Before she dozes off behind the wheel while nearly choking on the diesel fumes of the bus right in front of her bumper. The bus that royally cut her off a half hour ago. The only thing keeping her awake is the intermittent honking of horns from drivers just as pissed as she is about being stuck in gridlock on Pembina Highway, where she has seen the late-afternoon dusk turn into early-evening darkness. A light dusting of snow is falling and has been falling ever since the noon hour. And once again, Winnipeggers, living in an icebox for half the year, have seemingly forgotten how to drive in the snow. *See flakes, hit the brakes.* She hasn't moved more than a block or two over the last half hour. She is increasingly jealous of those people on the sidewalk who pass by and disappear from view. They're trudging along, ever so slowly climbing up and around the snowbanks. Even on such a major thoroughfare, they don't plow the sidewalks any better than they do the road. But at least they are moving and getting to where they're going. They're not trapped in a virtual jail cell like she is. Though it would mean freezing her ass off and falling down a few times, she is tempted to join them. Just shut off the engine and get out. The hell with the car. Even if it is well heated. She isn't that far from home. But then the bus in front of her pulls ahead a few inches. And she does the same. As does the driver behind her. Maybe things will start moving a little better now, she thinks. At least she hopes. She can now see a traffic light off in the distance. The likely cause of the backlog. Seems like there's at least one per kilometer on every street in Winnipeg. There's no problem city engineers can't solve without a traffic light, so it seems. It is red. That's why there was a little bit of movement. Every time she's stuck in traffic like this, cars seemingly move only when the light is red.

Lack of sleep is causing Sierra to grow increasingly agitated as the ever-so-brief sign of progress grinds to a halt just as quickly as it started as the light turns green. She balls her hand into a fist and pounds it on the steering wheel. She is ready to cry. She hasn't slept since getting assigned to the case. The couple of times she dozed off during the morning meeting after giving a brief update didn't count. She hoped Andrea didn't notice. But the hell if she did. Maybe then, she'd have given her some more help. Bring someone in to relieve her. She's not a doctor, where they make you stay up for days at a time when you're doing your residency. They'll pay her plenty for the OT, of course. That won't be a problem. It never is. But that doesn't give them the right to flog her like a rented mule. She'd give the team a more complete rundown on the investigation tomorrow morning. Once she got a full night's sleep. That is, assuming she won't have to bunk down in the back seat of her Ford Taurus. And assuming she won't be up half the night fighting with Victoria. Maybe Sierra will get lucky and she won't be home. *Who knows, maybe she's found herself someone new and moved out.*

Her job would have been made a whole lot easier if only they had surveillance cameras on the property. Everyone's got them these days, and it's not like they couldn't afford it. Wouldn't have even set them back that much even if money were tight. But sadly, when she asked, the answer was no. They had been talking about it, Dr. Klein said. That's as far as it went. Which didn't help Sierra or Leah much now.

Inside the house, there wasn't much out of the ordinary. Upstairs, the bedroom was a bit messy, as Dr. Klein had indicated, but nothing looked to be missing. Sierra even found Leah's passport hidden away in one of the drawers. She couldn't have been planning to go too far. The bed was in pristine condition and didn't even look like anyone had been sitting on it. Starting to feel like a zombie, Sierra was tempted to lie down on it and catch a few winks. But she still had a job to do. And it was still a potential crime scene.

Back on the main floor, all the door frames looked intact and there were no broken windows. She also looked at the locks. No signs of forced entry. Everything looked as it should. Just to cover all the bases, she went down to the basement. It was completely finished, of course. Complete with a thick shag carpet, a long bar with dark mahogany bar paneling and a marble top, and a game room featuring a pool table and dart board. Not to mention a big-screen TV. Bigger than the one she's got. Of course, it doesn't get much use these days with both her and Victoria on the go. Again, little out of the ordinary. But as she turned to head back upstairs, she noticed the door to the electrical panel was slightly ajar, so she gently pried it open with her flashlight. And as soon as she did, she recoiled and coughed a few times. As she should have expected, it was filled with dust and cobwebs. She wanted to shut the door right away, but the sight of a small beige box not more than a couple of inches square caught her attention. There were tiny red and green wires connected to it, each no thicker than a fingernail. She figured it wasn't for cable TV. Even she knew those wires were thicker. Maybe they were phone wires, she thought. But as she looked more carefully, she noticed how the dust and cobwebs around the small box had been wiped up. Like someone had been there recently. *Why? And why just there?* So when she got back upstairs, she asked Dr. Klein about it. He said there had been plenty of outages with the landline. Almost every two or three months, he said. Like clockwork. It had gotten so bad that every time he picks up the phone and gets a dial tone, he's surprised. *So that's why.*

Sierra then talked to Priscilla, their housekeeper. She was a small little thing. Almost as tiny as Sierra. Thin, but not too thin. Long black hair tied up at the back. She's got the face of a 50-year-old, but she probably isn't a day over 30. *Hard living in the Philippines, I guess.* She seemed afraid. Maybe because English isn't her first language or even her second language. Or because she's not in the country legally. As the two of them sat down opposite each other in the study, Sierra thought about reassuring her that she was not with immigration. She wasn't going to put her in handcuffs and send her back to the Philippines. But she decided to hold off. See how things went first.

As Sierra suspected, the hairs on the back of Priscilla's neck practically stood on end the second she identified herself as a police officer. Much as Sierra liked impressing people by using her title, she deliberately didn't call herself a detective to avoid freaking Priscilla out even more. Sierra first asked when she last saw Leah. "When I leave that night. Mrs. Leah says she want to talk to me next day. She seem a little mad."

"Why was she mad? Was anything wrong?"

"Not that I know, Mrs. Seera."

It's Sierra. But I guess that's close enough.

"Do you think she might have been mad at Dr. Klein?"

"Oh, no. Mrs. Leah and Dr. Klein, I never see them mad. Dr. Klein real good to her. They really good to kids too. Always take them places. Hockey games. Soccer games. Lots of things they do."

Just because you don't see them angry at each other, doesn't mean they're not. Some guys can be real good actors.

After asking if anything else was unusual, Sierra got to her main point. The spot in the kitchen. Priscilla said she didn't know a thing about it. "No, Mrs. Seera, I don't go there."

Well, someone went there. But who?

When Sierra got back from the meeting the following morning, she sent someone to check around the grounds while she went out back. Now that she had fetched her winter boots and changed into some long pants. And a heavier parka. Temps hadn't been above –25 for a couple of weeks. The howling winds out of the north made it feel like –80. She did see some tracks leading to the back door coming from around the side of the house. Didn't look too recent, though it was hard to tell because they were partially filled in with the day-old snow and the drifting. More than likely, it was someone reading the meter, which was right by the door. Sierra was still amazed that they still did that. Why they didn't have a more modern system where the readings were taken remotely was beyond her.

Even if it wasn't the meter reader, it was probably just the kids running around. Maybe they were busy making a snowman. Or snowperson. Even she had to admit that the habit of using gender-specific language was hard to break. There was probably a big one in front of the house. With a long carrot for a nose.

Climbing up onto the snow-covered deck, she carefully made her way around the hot tub to the railing to get a good view of the back yard and out to the river. She sure wasn't about to go trudging through the waist-deep snow out there. But even if she were so inclined, there was no need. Clearly, no one had been out there, least of all Leah. Sure, according to Dr. Klein, Leah was tiny. Just like Sierra. For all she knew, Leah could be buried under all that snow. But aside from a few squirrel tracks, the snow was in pristine condition. Probably no one had been out there since the first snow fell in late October. The scene was as pretty as a postcard. Maybe it wasn't appropriate under the circumstances, but she couldn't help but dig out her phone and snap a picture.

Not long after she went back inside the house, the grunt she sent out to look around the grounds came running in, huffing and puffing, saying he found something in the front yard at the far edge of the property. So after thawing out, finishing her coffee and getting down the last of her strawberry vanilla donut, a poor substitute for a proper breakfast, she bundled up once again and headed back outside. Not that she was anxious to go back out in the cold and freeze her ass off again. She'd certainly be willing to take his word for it, whatever he found that was so damned important. But she had to. She was, after all, in charge of the investigation. And someone's life was potentially on the line. So she had to make the effort. And a hell of an effort it was. She was wiped out long before she got halfway out there. *Couldn't they have shoveled a pathway? Even right near the fence, the snow was knee deep.* But when she finally got to the edge of the property, she saw a big crater in the middle of all that white stuff right by the fence, along with some deep tracks leading to the back of the house.

Hmmm.

Then the grunt pointed out a spot high up on the fence. It was too high up for her to see, but when she climbed up on the lower railing, she could definitely see the red spots. Had to be blood, she thought. And it was. The crime scene techs even confirmed it was human after she got back to the office. *Could prove useful when they get a suspect. If they get a suspect.*

The discovery left her with more questions than answers as she went over her thoughts on the way back to the house. Where she could thaw out once again. And catch her breath while the rest of the team did all the dirty work outside as she supervised from the comfort of the Kleins' heated mansion. The snow was so deep there it couldn't have been the kids playing. It had to have been an adult. An adult who cut himself scaling the fence, fell over in the snow, then made his way over to the house. Her theory was that it was most likely a break-in attempt. Residential break-ins were like a cottage industry in Winnipeg. You can't really call yourself a true Winnipegger unless your home had been broken into at least once. It was especially bad in rich neighborhoods like this. It was hardly a surprise when Dr. Klein told her their home had been broken into a couple of times. Whose hasn't, he said. In this case, the punk might have thought the coast was clear after seeing Dr. Klein and the kids take off, only to get a rude surprise when he saw there was still someone at home. Yet there were no signs of a struggle. But maybe she opened the front door for him, thinking her husband had forgotten something, and didn't bother checking to see who was at the door before opening it. Wouldn't be the first time such a thing has happened. Years ago, Sierra's neighbor made that mistake. Thugs forced their way inside, then bound and gagged them before making off with all their valuables and completely ransacking the house. Perhaps the same thing happened in this case, she thought. Maybe the punk got spooked and decided to kidnap her or something. Tie her up, stuff her in her own car and take her somewhere. The punk's gotta figure a family that lives around here's worth plenty and that Leah would probably command more in ransom than anything he'd get out of the house. But until they get a ransom demand, they can't possibly know. Dr. Klein said the missing Mercedes had a GPS tracker, but they can't get a trace on it.

Last known location is the garage. *How helpful.*

Before leaving to go back to the office, she had a couple of other grunts canvass the neighborhood. See if any of the neighbors saw or heard anything or knew of something going on at the house. Anything. But those who were home didn't have much to say. Most didn't even know who lived there. *Real tight-knit community.* Aside from the normal comings and goings and the occasional party, there wasn't anything out of the ordinary. She would get another unit to make the rounds this evening when people got back from work in the hopes of getting more responses at the door, but she wasn't terribly hopeful.

Right after the meeting, she had someone check into Leah's cell phone and when she got back to the office, she had access to her voice mail and call logs from the past couple of weeks. There was no luck in tracing the phone itself. It was off and had been ever since the night Leah disappeared. Just like with the GPS tracker, the last known location was her house. There was only one voice mail message: someone at Leah's workplace wondering where she was. She had apparently been expected in a meeting today. There were a lot of calls to go through, but most of the activity was with her family and people connected with her work. Nothing raised an eyebrow.

Sierra had no additional insight after calling a number of family members. No one had heard from Leah and there was no hint of any marital problems whatsoever. Quite the contrary, everyone pointed to them as the seemingly ideal couple. A modern-day version of the Waltons.

After a late lunch, Sierra got back in her Taurus and headed for the PTC, where Leah worked. Each one of her colleagues was deeply concerned, of course. Especially in light of the incident in the parking garage that Dr. Klein told her about soon after she'd gotten to the house. Sierra already had someone looking into getting the surveillance footage. Maybe someone had been stalking her and followed her home, she thought. Naturally, Sierra asked the usual questions. Had anyone heard from Leah? Had she been acting strangely? Was she having some kind of a midlife crisis? Was anyone following her? Negative on all counts. But she still had to ask. You never know. They did recommend talking to Shirley Bender, a close friend of Leah's who was off-site setting up a new production at one of their other theaters. So Sierra got back into her Taurus and drove down the street to go see her. No way she was going to walk outside in this weather even if it was just a couple of blocks. If her legs didn't freeze, she'd trip and fall on the ice. Why the city didn't clear the sidewalks better she had no idea. Just tossing out more sand doesn't help much. Not to mention that by taking her car, she couldn't get hit on by the bums. The cold gets most of them off the street, but not all of them.

Once inside the Ari Goldschmidt Theater, Sierra made her way through the dark main floor seating area, which felt colder than it did outside. *I know your budget is tight, but turn up the damned heat!* After finding the thermostat and cranking it up to a more comfortable 24 degrees, she followed the sound of hammers and drills toward a few stage hands working on some props. Sierra asked if they knew where to find Shirley, and all she got was a series of identical blank stares. Total deer in the headlights. But when she mentioned that Shirley was a production associate, one of them limply angled his thumb toward the back. *Gee, don't put yourself out, dude!* Down the hall, she finally found someone who seemed to know Shirley and pointed to a nearby office. There, she saw a plump, middle-aged woman—her mop of hair half her natural gray and the other half dyed dirty blond—seated at a desk with her head buried in a pile of papers, while munching on a Rice Krispies square and brushing the crumbs off the papers. Sierra noticed that the woman was dressed in a flashy gold top draped in a black cashmere wool wrap, an outfit she instantly took a liking to. It certainly wasn't her size. *That woman has had a few too many of those Rice Krispies squares.* But she made a mental note to do everything she could to steer the conversation they were about to have to finding out where she got it. *With any luck, they'll have a smaller size.*

Sierra gently knocked on the door before going in.

"Hello, I'm looking for Shirley Bender."

"You must be from the police," said Shirley, while keeping her head down, fussing over the papers in front of her. *Sorry to trouble you, but you know, your friend and colleague might be dead.*

"Actually, yes. I'm Detective Sierra Kowalski with the Homicide Unit. Do you have a few minutes?"

"Don't suspect you have any good news. Been worried sick ever since I heard Leah was missing," said Shirley, who took the card Sierra offered and studied it for a bit before motioning for her to take a seat, still preoccupied with those papers. Only when Sierra pulled out the chair and sat down did Shirley finally take off her glasses and look Sierra in the eyes.

"Sorry," explained Shirley. "I need to get this done. We've got a big production debuting in a couple of days. The show must go on, you know. Leah always said that." *She used past tense when referring to Leah. Slip of the tongue? Or does she know something?*

"No problem," said Sierra. "I understand." Sierra used to go to the theater herself. She had seen a number of plays right in that building, in fact. Back then, it was just called The Annex. She would get discounted tickets through the Faculty of Arts and go with a group of classmates. Then they'd go clubbing later and talk about the play. Most often, they wouldn't get back to their dorm until two or three in the morning. Completely wasted. Good thing they didn't have drug testing at the U of W. Those were the days. Before she got super-duper busy with her new job.

Sierra asked Shirley the same questions she did of the others. Shirley said she hadn't seen Leah since Monday. The last day anyone had seen her. Hadn't heard from her since. Texted her multiple times over the last couple of days, but still nothing.

Sierra then asked if Shirley knew of anyone who might want to harm Leah. If anyone was following her. Anything like that.

"Uhhhh, no. I don't think so."

I don't **think** *so? You know more. Cough it up, girl!*

"Are you sure, Shirley?"

Try the gentle approach.

Shirley put her head down.

"It's probably nothing," she mumbled.

Sierra reached out to put her hand on Shirley's.

"Shirley, I hope it is nothing. But Leah is missing. Maybe something's happened to her. Maybe not. I really hope not. But if you have something to tell us, however small, we need to know."

The torment was written all over Shirley's face.

"By the way, I love your outfit." *I just had to ask her. Besides, it might butter her up.* "Do you mind me asking where you got it?"

Shirley tries to force a smile.

"Maude Sterling. St. Vital Center," she says in a weak voice.

Damn! A plus-size store.

Keeping her hand on Shirley's, Sierra pressed for more.

"Please, Shirley. It's important."

"Leah swore me to secrecy. She thought she was being paranoid."

"Please, go on," said Sierra after a lengthy pause.

"She said Aaron would have her committed. I swear she was only half-joking. It was her ex-husband. Mitch. Can't even remember his last name now," said Shirley, shaking like a leaf. "Look at me, I'm a wreck."

Hmmm, there's that name again. I wanted to talk to him anyway.

"It's all right, Shirley. Leah would understand."

After gathering herself, Shirley continued.

"She always thought he was watching her. I suppose you know about the restraining order and all."

"Yes, Dr. Klein mentioned it."

Maybe he hadn't been leaving her alone after all.

"Even though she never actually saw him again after that, Leah always had that feeling he was around. Somewhere. Lurking in the shadows. Keeping an eye on her. Following her. I don't know if there was anything to it. But Leah sure thought there was. I suppose it's understandable under the circumstances. From what she told me about him, the guy was a real psycho."

After a pause while Sierra was busily taking notes, Shirley offered another thought.

"You know, it could all be nothing. Mitch could be in Timbuktu for all I know. He probably hasn't seen Leah in years. I don't know. Maybe Leah was in a car accident or something and they just haven't found her. Or something like what happened with Sheila. She's one of our former colleagues who—"

"Dr. Klein told me about her. Such a tragedy."

"Yeah, none of us have forgotten that. And especially now with Leah. Brings it all back like it was yesterday," said Shirley as her voice tailed off, tears forming in her eyes. She stopped to blow her nose with a blast that nearly shook the room.

Sierra sat back and let Shirley regather herself.

"Was there anything more, Shirley?" she asked while handing Shirley another Kleenex. She had already gone through three of them and the snot was still pouring out.

"I don't think so," mumbled Shirley as the last of the sniffles at least appeared to be behind her.

There might be more, but she's too emotionally spent right now. For sure, I won't be able to get anything more out of her today. I'll follow up tomorrow or the next day. Or, with any luck, maybe she'll call me. And in the meantime, I need to check into this psycho ex-husband a little more.

"Well, you have my card, and if you think of anything else, please don't hesitate to call," said Sierra, again gently putting her hand on Shirley's as she got up to leave. And instantly regretting it. As well as the decision not to pack a bottle of hand sanitizer in her purse. She would have needed every drop of it to wash all that icky snot off.

Sierra certainly did need to follow up on Mitch Schubert. But that would have to wait until tomorrow. She has no more energy left. And she's cranky as hell. Without any sleep, she's been running on little more than cappuccino all day long. Which was why she clocked out early for the day. But first, she needs to get out of jail. And if the gridlock on Pembina Highway doesn't break soon, she just might shut off the engine, crawl into the back seat, lie down and go to sleep.

Chapter 9

The Doctor
Thursday, January 18, 6:58 PM

Dr. Raymond Cho winds up another miserable day by locking the door to his office, wishing he didn't have to come back. Spending his time poking his finger up assholes and listening to people bellyache about their trivial problems wasn't what he signed up for when he decided to follow in his father's footsteps and go into med school. He thought being a doctor would be more glamorous. That's why he spent eight rough years at the U of M and another three being abused during his residency. Suffering through those brutal 36-hour shifts. Sure, he's raking in gobs of money, just like his father did. Which is nice. Wouldn't have that three-storey mansion on the river in Fort Richmond without it, not to mention the vacation property in Costa Rica. Just down the street from the premier, who spends two or three months of the year down there. There's no way he'd be able to make it through these hellish Manitoba winters without it. The cold is absolutely inhuman. But some days, he wonders if all the money's really worth it. Surely there was something else he could have done instead that would pay half-decently.

Almost as bad is all the paperwork. Some days he spends more time filling out forms than with his patients. *Bloody government!* It's no wonder he hardly ever gets home before eight. It's been months since was last home in time for dinner. He hardly sees his children anymore. Even when he's home on the weekends, they're out and about and often out of the house before he gets up in the morning. These days, "Daddy" is just the name of a human ATM who pays the bills and signs the checks.

After locking the door, he walks across the hall and tugs on the sliding steel mesh door to the pharmacy that closed a couple of hours ago. They had to put it in last year because they were getting robbed almost every other week. *Damn, it's unlocked! Again!* He's reminded Olivia, the pharmacist, about it several times in the last few weeks. But she just doesn't listen. It's as if she doesn't give a shit anymore. So what if the place gets hit again. It's not coming out of her pocket. It's coming out of his because the last two times they got hit when the door was unlocked, the insurance company refused to pay the claim. He's going to have to look for another pharmacist. The U of M is spitting out graduates like popcorn. Hire one of them instead. One that cares. Just a little. At least make the junkies work for their haul. In the meantime, he's got to lock it up himself. But after fumbling through his pockets, he realizes he must have left the spare key in his other coat. The one he changed out of this morning and left in his car to drop off at the dry cleaners after one of his patients barfed all over it. He'll have to go and fetch it first before setting the alarm and locking up for the night.

He hasn't had a chance to look out the window since the sun went down, so he doesn't know if more snow has fallen. There was certainly enough of it yesterday. He was stuck in traffic for over an hour for a drive that normally takes him just over 10 minutes. It was nuts. All he can do is hope. And hope that the plows have come. They hadn't been out overnight. When he came in this morning, Pembina Highway was still only barely passable. All the way, he was sliding around trying his best to stay within the ruts and not run into another car. Whatever the case, he knows it will be damned cold outside, so before he steps out the rear door to where his Beemer is parked, he zips up his parka and wraps his dark red woolen scarf around his neck. The scarf that his mother knitted for him when he was a youngster during their first winter in Canada after their family emigrated from Hong Kong still means the world to him. Mom was always so horrified by the cold. "You'll catch your death out there," she would always say when she wrapped that scarf around his neck before he went outside.

After sending a short text to his wife telling her he's on his way, he turns the handle to the outside door. It turns easy enough, but it feels like there's a gorilla the size of King Kong leaning against the door. *Must be the wind. It whips around the alley all the time.* He puts his shoulder into it and manages to push it open ever so slowly. And after struggling to give himself enough of a gap to squeeze through the door frame, he gets slammed with a blast of Arctic air. Sure enough, he was right. But he's at least relieved that it's not snowing and that there's only a light dusting of snow on his Beemer. With any luck, he won't have to spend too much time scraping the ice off the windows.

An instant after the door slams shut behind him, he is startled by a punch to the left side of his face, knocking him off balance as his head bounces off the back of the brick wall next to the door. He is dazed and disoriented. He may have a slight concussion. He feels a throbbing pain in his cheekbone. He can still taste the cold leather from the glove covering the fist that also split his lip and smashed his glasses. Trying to regain his footing, he feels something sharp slicing through the scarf protecting his Adam's apple from the cold. The knife has broken the skin and is penetrating deep into his trachea. It feels heavy. It's not a switchblade. It's probably a big kitchen knife. Probably like the one Christine used to slice up the roast they had for dinner tonight. As she normally does, she probably put aside a portion for him to pop in the microwave when he gets home. But he now knows those are leftovers he will not see. They will probably go to waste as Christine and the kids won't feel much like eating. Except maybe for Brian. Brian always eats like a horse. Even planning his father's funeral won't diminish his appetite. No doubt the kid will become a master chef and open up his own restaurant someday.

Dr. Cho is desperately gasping for air. The scarf, saturated with his own warm blood, feels like a collar tightening around his neck. Losing strength, he falls to the ground. Slumped on the icy pavement with his back against the brick wall, he can see only a faint glimmer of the two-watt bulb hanging above the rear door.

It is the last sight he sees before he blacks out.

Chapter 10

The Morning Meeting
Friday, January 19, 9:31 AM

Sierra can only keep looking up at the clock and wondering how much longer this insufferable meeting will go on. And how much longer she can stay awake. Lattes and cappuccinos can only do so much with all the irregular hours she's been putting in of late. Not to mention that she's not getting much sleep during the brief times when she's home. Last night, for example, she was up half the night fighting with Victoria. No doubt the neighbors were having a ball listening to them scream at each other at the top of their lungs. They can probably hear everything through those paper-thin walls in their condo. That bitch made Sierra so mad that she wanted to grab that mop of long blond hair and tear it out by the roots. *Let's see how popular Vickie C is with a bald head full of ugly red scratches and scabs!* Instead, she settled for smashing the glass pitcher Victoria likes so much against the wall before turning her back and bunking down on the sofa once again. Damned if she was going to clean up the mess. Let Victoria take care of it. It was her fault. But even though Sierra had pulled the covers over her head, the bitch still kept screaming. Wouldn't let her get a wink of sleep. What she really should have done was go to that luxury five-star hotel just down the street. After all the shit she's been putting up with at home and on the job lately, she's earned the right to pamper herself a little.

Normally, Sierra is loath to take even one donut during the meetings. They just go right to her hips and she does watch her figure. Unlike so many of the women in the office who look like they work out at the Dairy Queen. Whenever they waddle down the hallways, it probably registers on the Richter scale. The worst part is how they try to fit into outfits, like, ten times too small. Even though the seams are practically bursting, they'll do everything to say they're a size six or eight. But in the vain hope that it might help keep her awake, Sierra reaches for a second donut, raising the eyebrows of a couple of her female colleagues around the table. The first two boxes are empty, so she has to dig into the rightmost of the three on the table, where there are still a couple left inside. Not that she was paying attention too carefully, but she suspects Norm has probably inhaled the first two and half the third. Norm is, like, 500 pounds and has a big beer belly. And he always reeks of smoke and booze. Like he just walked out of a bar. Andrea usually brings only two dozen donuts, but today, she brought three. No doubt because she knew the meeting would go longer as a result of the new case she got word about sometime last night.

As she takes her first bite of the strawberry vanilla donut, she turns back toward her colleague Ken Stammers, who has spent the last couple of years in Homicide after 16 years in the gang unit. In his late 50s, he's as tall as those basketball players, rail thin and seemingly always sporting three-day-old salt-and-pepper stubble on that weather-beaten face of his accented by his trademark horn-rimmed glasses. He looks just like her seventh-grade history teacher. The one who gave her a D on her project on the War of 1812. She still remembers how she went home and cried for hours. She just couldn't understand how he could have been so heartless. She worked so hard on it. It's probably why she's never quite taken to Ken. That and how he always talks down to her. Like a real know-it-all. Andrea says he's like that to everyone and not to take it so personally. Whatever. At least he'll be retiring soon. One less member of the old guard she'll have to contend with. Luckily it was Ken and not Sierra who drew the short straw last night and has been filling the group in on all the details for the last half hour or so. Turns out some doctor got his throat cut behind a pharmacy on Pembina Highway. Dr. Raymond Cho was his name. General practitioner, Asian, 47 years old, wife and three children. Born in Hong Kong. Family came to Canada when he was seven. Clean record. Even though she's never been in the place before, Sierra knows the building well since she passes by it every day on the way to and from work. The wife was the one who called it in. She was worried after he didn't come home. A couple of hours earlier, he texted her saying he was on his way. So she went to the office to check on him. Found him lying in the alley next to the back door covered in blood, not more than a few feet from his car.

Inside, the pharmacy right across from Dr. Cho's office had been broken into and a bunch of drugs were taken. Sierra certainly agreed with Andrea's assessment that it had all the signs of a typical junkie hit. The doctor was just in the wrong place at the wrong time. Happens all the time. Andrea sees no reason for a lengthy investigation and told Ken to wrap it up quickly. Our case load is pretty heavy right now, she said. But Ken thinks there's more to it. As always. It's like he's got to impress us with his wealth of knowledge. Show us neophytes that he's the alpha male in the room.

When he went in with the crime scene techs, Ken said he noticed that it looked like the areas behind and around the drug counter had been trashed almost at random. So what, Andrea asked? The perp was probably stoned out of his mind. But Ken said when he's seen cases like this, it's done more professionally. They're looking for specific drugs and know where to find them. Oxycontin most often. They don't take the time to smash up the aisle with aspirin and baby food. To him, it was as if they were out to target this specific pharmacy. Maybe the pharmacist gave someone the wrong drugs or something. He wants to go through the files to check for anyone who may have had a gripe with the pharmacy or even the doctor, but Andrea says that could take, like, forever and they don't have the resources to pursue a wild goose chase. But after Ken kept pressing, she did finally relent and gave him a few days to look into it a little more. Then just round up the usual suspects, as Norm said. One of them will squeak. They always do. Even if they're not guilty.

As Sierra takes another bite, Ken tells the group the autopsy will likely be done early next week, but one hardly needed a medical degree to determine the cause of death. His throat had been slit from end to end and if that didn't get him, the various knife wounds on his face and his chest did. Some sicko really went to town on the poor bugger. Front, back, everywhere. Left nothing to chance. Carved him up like a Christmas turkey. The scene was a real mess. One of the worst he's seen in his career. He somehow managed to hold it together, but one of the newbies on the forensics team dry-heaved right next to the body. Just like that quarterback did in the huddle during the Super Bowl one year. So now everyone's calling him Donovan, after the quarterback. Captain Dry-Heave.

All the talk of puking makes Sierra want to cough up the remaining bits of the latest bite of donut in her mouth. But after getting the last of it down, she asks if it could have been the wife. *Marital problems, perhaps?* Though Ken summarily dismissed her idea, it was a theory she was still hung up on with her own case after spending much of yesterday talking to and checking up on Leah's ex, Mitch Schubert. Sierra found him easily enough from his LinkedIn profile, which showed he was a sales rep in the Winnipeg office of a big multinational company. When she called him up, he said he's been under the weather lately and hasn't been out of his apartment much for the last few days. Doctor's orders, he said. Sierra later called the property manager of Schubert's block, who confirmed that his car is buried under a couple of feet of snow and hasn't been out of the lot for a while. He also said he hadn't seen Schubert recently. "The guy's always out and about. Coming and going all the time. But not lately. Thought he was out of town, to tell you the truth," he said. Schubert had gone on and on about how badly he was feeling. Stuffed-up head. Sick to his stomach. Couldn't keep much food down. Throwing up all the time. Didn't even feel like getting out of bed half the time. "It's just the flu, you know," he said. "Everyone in Winnipeg has it now or so it seems. Should have gotten the flu shot like my doctor said. But I'm, like, squeamish about needles and stuff. And I've been so busy with work and stuff. So I kind of forgot about it. And now I'm paying for it."

Once he finished bellyaching about all his health problems that had been keeping him laid up, Sierra asked where he was on Monday night, the night his ex disappeared. He said he was probably holed up in his unit. "Probably just vegging out in front of the TV, as best as I can remember. If I had even been awake. Heck, even if I had been feeling great, it was too bloody cold to go anywhere," he said with a laugh. But just as Sierra was finishing scribbling down her notes and preparing to ask him more about his ex-wife, Schubert suddenly remembered where he was that night. "I went downstairs to visit Tommy, that's right. How could I have forgotten? We hung out for a while. Played video games. As we usually do. Tommy's got a Nintendo system and no one knows Nintendo like Tommy. Of course he beat the pants off me again," he said. "Tommy is a little mentally challenged, walks with a peg leg and doesn't have many friends. But he gets around surprisingly well and is a fun guy to be around." Sierra found it a little strange, but she later followed up with Tommy at the number Schubert gave her and he confirmed the story. "Oh yeah, he here with me. All night," Tommy said. "Mitch is here all the time. Mitch is my friend." When asked how he remembered Monday night specifically, Tommy replied, "Someone won a trip to Hawaii on *Wheel of Fortune*. Sure wish I could go there. Play on the beach. Lot better than here. Don't think they get too much snow in Hawaii." *The guy's got a point!*

Schubert went on to say he couldn't even remember when he had last seen Leah. "I do hope she's OK though," he said. "But I wouldn't worry. She's always been a little flighty. When we were married, she took off a couple of times without telling anyone. I was freaking out the first time. But she came back and acted as though nothing ever happened. So when it happened the second time, it was no big whoop. She'll probably turn up in a day or two. Just needs to find peace with the universe or something. You know how those artsy-fartsy types are. Always seem to be in the middle of a spiritual crisis."

Funny, Dr. Klein never mentioned anything like that.

"Your marriage didn't exactly end amicably, Mr. Schubert. Leah even had to get a restraining order against you."

"Oh please, detective. Call me Mitch."

"All right, Mitch." *Trying to butter me up.*

"You know, I'll be the first to admit that I took the breakup really hard. Even though we had been at each other's throats for some time, I was still head over heels in love with her, you know," he said with a laugh. "Despite all the problems we'd been having, I was completely blindsided when she packed up and left me. I couldn't believe it. I was totally devastated. I thought my whole world had fallen apart. Try as I might, I just couldn't deal with it. So I lashed out. I was obsessed. I kept following her. I know now it wasn't the right thing to do. She hurt me deeply. It was like she drove a dagger through my heart. Then when she got the restraining order, it only infuriated me even more. I wanted to get back at her. It was especially tough when she took up with another man, that dentist. But then I went for anger management counseling. And it really helped me to move on. Honestly, I haven't thought about Leah at all in the last few years. Until recently, of course, when I heard the news that she was missing."

Listening to his diatribe, Sierra wasn't sure what to make of him. On the surface, he sure sounded nice enough on the phone. But maybe too nice. He is, after all, a salesman. She needed to keep her mind open and go to work on him a little more. Which she did. And from the court records she checked into before making the call, the dude sounded seriously creepy. Not just from the Leah case, but the priors he had for harassment and uttering threats against another guy. Yet it all took place a long time ago. And so far, everything about his story checked out, including the part of his being off work sick. Right after hanging up with him, she called his employer, who confirmed that he hadn't been at work all week. Sick leave was all the HR lady could say. Confidentiality and all. Sierra checked into him a little more and found that his uncle is a prominent dermatologist with a hair replacement clinic. *I knew the name sounded familiar!* Dr. Earl Schubert is well known for doing hairpieces for all sorts of high-profile clients including celebrities, politicians and hockey players.

Whatever the case with Mitch, he and Dr. Klein are about all they have as far as suspects are concerned, so Andrea advised putting them both under surveillance and keeping our eyes and ears open. Andrea would also look into getting a warrant to get their call logs and tap into their phones. Might just get lucky.

Just when Ken seems to be winding down his update, Corazon pipes up. She is a new Canadian who emigrated from the Philippines about five years ago and got her posting in Homicide just after Sierra did. Desperate to make an impression, she always has to interject something at every meeting, however stupid it may be. She's never content to let a super-boring monologue die. So often Sierra has wanted to just slap her upside the head, and no more so than right now. But Ken is taking care of it. Belittling her and her suggestion that it was racially motivated by someone targeting people of Asian heritage. Right in front of everyone. Her face is turning beet red, and right after the meeting, she'll probably make a beeline for the ladies' room to bawl her eyes out. Part of Sierra feels sorry for her. In a way. She certainly knows the feeling. She's been there a few times herself. But it serves Corazon right. Maybe she'll finally get it through her thick skull to keep her big mouth shut.

Strictly speaking, Sierra has to grudgingly admit that Ken was kind of hard on her. Corazon wasn't *that* far off base. There might even be something to it given how prevalent racism is in Winnipeg. But Sierra is pissed off. At her job. At the cold. At Victoria. At the traffic. At just about everything. And right now, especially at Corazon. Sierra just wants the meeting to end. And for the day to be over. So she can start her weekend. Maybe if the roads aren't too bad, she can make an impromptu three-hour drive south to Grand Forks for some cross-border shopping. Just grab her passport and go. Alone. Victoria probably wouldn't even notice that she's gone. So Sierra can't help but smile as she sees Corazon's eyes begin to well up. She deserves it for keeping Sierra in jail.

With Ken having finished his beatdown of Corazon, Andrea finally wraps up the meeting. Sierra feels like applauding. This time Corazon keeps quiet. *For sure, she's too bloody embarrassed to pipe up now.* So as the group fights over the remaining donuts and Corazon does a lightning-quick exit stage left, Sierra gets up and heads back to her desk. There's a missing person to find.

Dead or alive.

Chapter 11

Brent

Saturday, January 20, 6:42 AM

After putting the last of their bags in the back of his shiny, new metallic blue Mercedes SUV, Brent Jackson gets behind the wheel and listens to the engine purring like a kitten before giving Stacey a big wet kiss on the lips. Truth be known, he'd much rather have stayed in bed with her this morning than get up at such an ungodly hour. She's so much easier on the eyes than Karen was. Sometimes he can't believe he stayed with that old hag and her children so long. *God, she turned out to be such a miserable bitch.* And Stacey looks even better now since she went from a C cup to a DD. Not that she didn't look utterly fabulous before, mind you. But he's getting full value on his dollar, that's for sure. Dr. Bernstein did a fantastic job. No scars or anything. They're just perfect. And he'll be able to see a lot more of those new and improved curves when she's strutting around in a tiny bikini on the beach in Jamaica. She's such a flirt. It's one of the many things he loves about her. Always fun to be around. Laughing and giggling all the time. She makes him feel like a kid again. It's been that way ever since they've been together, even before they were married this past summer. He's wanted to tie the knot for over a year now, but he first had to wait until his divorce was final. Everything would have gone so much smoother and faster if Karen hadn't put up such a stink. It was pathetic. She denies it, of course, but the only logical explanation was that she was jealous of Stacey. Karen only wishes she had a figure like hers. But then when it was finally all over, Stacey wanted to wait until after her high school graduation. Which was rational.

He still can't figure out why his parents are so upset about his relationship with Stacey. *They didn't even come to the wedding, for crying out loud!* He even offered to pay their way to Niagara Falls, but they still said no. So what if there's a big age difference. With two mature adults, 33 years is nothing. It's how young you are at heart. And he's hardly robbing the cradle. She's of legal age. She's got her own health card. She can vote. She can even drink legally now. Even though there's no way in a million years they'd admit it, he thinks they're still sore about him changing his name years ago. They nearly hit the roof when he first told them. "You're dishonoring your ancestors," they said. "It's an insult to your entire family who came here from Poland with nothing and worked so hard to make something of themselves here in Canada." But Jackson is so much easier than Jankowski. It was a business decision all the way. Surely his ancestors would understand. But his parents just can't see that.

Before they can feel the sand between their toes, however, they first have to get to the airport. The plane isn't going to wait and it's a 10-hour flight with a layover in Toronto. So he puts the car in gear and pulls out of their triple-car garage into the early-morning twilight, leaving her silver Lexus and his black Jaguar behind. Out of the corner of his eye, he notices her sneaking a look back at the Lexus. How she just loves it. Sometimes he thinks she loves it more than she loves him. Especially this summer when she was able to put the top down. She looked like a little girl with a new play set. It was the perfect wedding present. Besides the huge ring, of course. He loves making her happy. Because she makes him happy.

Turning out onto Henderson Highway, he punches their destination into the GPS. Not that he needs the help. It's more out of habit. As a frequent business traveler, he knows the way to the airport like the back of his hand. But in this case, he's glad he did. There's a warning. The bridge at the Perimeter Highway over the Red River is all in red. Meaning it's closed. Must be an accident or something. *There's certainly enough of them. Understandable given all the ice and snow on the roads.* So he'll have to use the Lockport Bridge to get over the river instead.

With one eye on his squeeze while exchanging sweet nothings with her, he makes his way across the bridge and turns south. Rather than continuing straight ahead as the GPS advises, he opts to turn west at Highway 67 right by the old stone fort at Lower Fort Garry. He suspects the cops might have the Perimeter blocked all the way to Highway 8, so he'll follow Highway 67 to Highway 7, then turn south and head into the city from there. *Best to avoid all the shemozzle on the Perimeter.*

After making the turn, he is relieved by the sight of grader tracks and the fresh piles of snow on both sides of the highway. It means the highway has been plowed recently. *They probably did it overnight.* Not that the snow would present much of a challenge for his SUV. Ever since he bought it last year, it's breezed through all kinds of snowdrifts. The four-wheel drive feature proved to be worth every penny. But he knows this is not the time or the place to put it to the test. To borrow a line from *Predator*, if you get stuck out here, you're in a world of hurt. Something he knows all too well, having had to crisscross the province at all times of the year to meet clients. Once, he had to make the eight-hour drive north to Thompson. Way up near the Arctic Circle. *Bloody igloo country.* Halfway up there, his old Dodge van broke down. Ended up being stuck in the frozen tundra overnight until help came. Darned near froze to death.

The sight of the desolate, snow-covered prairie stretching as far as the eye can see chills him to the bone. So he reaches over to turn the heat up to full blast. Stacey sure doesn't mind. Despite being all wrapped up in that mink coat he bought her for Christmas, she's still shivering. Good thing the only white stuff they'll be seeing for the next couple of weeks is the sand on the beach. Where they'll be frolicking and sipping pina coladas.

Thoughts of those sandy beaches and palm trees make it increasingly harder for him to keep his eyes on the road. And off Stacey. Imagining when she's out of that mink coat and in something a lot less confining. Good thing there hasn't been anyone else on the road as he's sure he's crossed the yellow line more than a few times. The last thing he needs is to get into an accident. Still, he can't resist glancing over to his right once again as she turns to face him. Giving him that naughty, seductive look as she puts her finger in her mouth and sucks on it gently. She places her free hand on his thigh. He begins to hyperventilate as she rubs it back and forth, moving ever closer to his crotch. *Oooooohhh, she's so good at this* . . .

As he veers off the road and onto the ice-covered gravel shoulder, out of the corner of his eye, he catches sight of a rickety old black pickup truck off in the distance pulling out from a side road. He snaps his head forward and jerks the SUV to the left. After swerving around, he eventually gets it back under control as the pickup gathers speed in the opposite lane heading their way. *Whew!* Finally back in control and headed due west, he casts a quick smile back at Stacey. *We'll pick this up later, babe!*

Less than a half mile ahead of them, the pickup begins to drift over the yellow line. Brent leans on his horn. *Bloody farmer. Wake up!* Not that Brent has any room to lecture anyone else, having just nearly driven his SUV into the ditch. But the truck continues to slowly drift over to their lane. Anger turns to concern as the distance between them closes. *Jesus Christ!* Brent keeps leaning on the horn, yet the truck is still picking up speed and is now straddling the yellow line. With a head-on collision only seconds away, Brent cannot help but think of the story his father told him about the time when he was driving a big rig out in rural Saskatchewan many years ago. Dad was on this deserted two-lane highway, probably not unlike the one Brent is on right now. A truck headed in the opposite direction began drifting over to his lane, barreling along at 60 or 70 miles an hour. No doubt the other driver, like the one in front of Brent, was falling asleep at the wheel. Dad had little time to make a potentially life-altering decision. Does he hit the ditch? Or does he go in the opposite lane and try to avoid him that way? Hoping the other driver didn't suddenly wake up and swing back into his own lane. Dad chose the latter option. It turned out to be the right call. The other driver kept drifting over, and Dad went around him and continued on as if nothing happened. Lived to tell the story. But he was always curious as to what happened with the other driver. Did he survive? Never saw anything in the news about it. Oh well. But now it's a case of like father, like son. Brent wants to do the same and swerve to his left to avoid the pickup, but it's holding course. Mostly in Brent's lane, but still partly straddling the yellow line. And there's not enough time. There's only a couple of car lengths between them now. The distance is closing much too fast to avoid a crash if he swerves left. So he has no choice. He can only go right. Straight into the snowy ditch. And pray the safety features work as advertised. Especially the airbags. He didn't pay much attention when the salesman told him it was the safest car on the road. He was far more interested in having the most luxurious car on the road. One that makes a statement. But those safety features mean everything now. That SOB better be right. Or Brent will kill the bastard. Assuming he gets out of this alive.

His hard right thankfully allows him to avoid the pickup, which has swerved away at the last second. *Why didn't that asshole wake up a few seconds earlier?* As he blows through the thick windrow of snow piled up alongside the shoulder, the impact sets off the front airbags. *Shit! There goes the trip now!* The airbag from the steering wheel violently throws Brent against the back of the seat, cracking his glasses and knocking them off his face. The SUV continues down the steep grade beyond the windrow at an awkward angle, and the left-side wheels begin to lift off the ground. As much as Brent tries to will it back, he is powerless to stop his Mercedes from rolling over onto the passenger's side. He cringes at the sound of metal crunching and glass breaking. It continues to roll until finally coming to a hard stop, with the SUV upside down at the bottom of the ditch.

Brent is sore. Badly disoriented. And after fumbling about to unhook his seat belt, his head hits the roof. *Ow! That hurt!* But otherwise, he feels little pain and there is movement in both his arms and legs. He is relieved knowing he has survived and probably not much the worse for wear. Sadly, he can't say the same for his Mercedes, but it can be replaced. That's what insurance is for. Maybe he'll get a different color next time. Bright red. He looks over to his left, however, and sees that Stacey has not been so lucky. The roof of the SUV is coated with her blood. He brushes aside some of her hair and sees that she's been tossed around like a rag doll. He realizes she must have taken off her seat belt when she was playing games with him on the highway. *Aww, babe!* He wants to get out, but he can't seem to find the button to unlock the door. *Never had to unlock the door when the car was upside down before.* He finally finds the latch, but the door doesn't budge. The front window doesn't look like a good option either. Even if he could pry his legs free and kick out the glass, it's butted against the bank of the ditch. He'll have to wait until the paramedics come with the Jaws of Life to extricate them. *Surely the bugger at least had the decency to stop and call 911.*

Then he smells smoke. And feels warm. Much too warm. Like he's leaning inside an oven. The temperature continues to rise as a pungent toxic stench and thick, black smoke fill the cabin. He is coughing up a storm, but his lungs are fighting a losing battle with the smoke. He knows he has to get out or he will die even before the flames envelop the SUV. In desperation, he flails his elbow against the driver's side window. It's his only chance. But he's running out of time. He keeps coughing. And coughing. The smoke has completely filled the cabin. He can hardly breathe.

He screams as the flames begin melting the seat behind him and his parka.
But no one can hear him.

Chapter 12

Two More
Saturday, January 20, 8:31 PM

After a long, hot shower, Mitch flops down on the couch and cracks open a beer. Then he grabs the remote and turns on the tube. Amid all the commotion, he had forgotten it was Saturday night. *Time for Hockey Night in Canada.* A Canadian tradition unlike any other. He hopes he can find a good game. After all he's been through over the past couple of days, he's certainly earned it. He flips around to see if the Habs are on. But they're not. Once again, it's just the Leafs. And he hates the Leafs. No, he despises the Leafs. So he slams his thumb down on the big red button and tosses the remote on the table in disgust. Maybe it's all for the best, he thinks. He can't be bothered to sit up watching hockey all night. He has no energy left. He needs to get to bed and try to get some sleep. He needs his rest. This is taking a hell of a toll on him.

This morning's escapade went without a hitch. Brent played right into his hands. Things couldn't have gone any smoother. All week long, he was bragging on the company bulletin board and all over social media about his getaway to Jamaica with his latest floozy. How he'll be enjoying fun in the sun while we're stuck here shivering in our igloos. Rubbing our noses in it. Even put the time of his flight on his Outlook calendar for all to see. Making it ridiculously simple for Mitch to set him up for the kill. Like taking candy from a baby. Just call in a bomb threat on the North Perimeter Bridge. Naturally, the cops were out there in a flash. They practically had half the force out there to shut most of the north end of the city down. They're so predictable. So easy to get the cops to do what you want in this town. Brent had practically no choice but to use Highway 67. It was only out on the open road where things could have gotten tricky because the traction was so poor. They had plowed it, but once again, all it did was expose the ice and make it like a skating rink. And the old pickup Mitch borrowed from a nearby farmer had bald tires. *Must be the one he uses to shuttle the migrant workers around. The Wetback Express.* Had a heck of a time getting it out of the driveway. Needed to pull it out with the big delivery truck he had stolen. Dude should seriously consider hiring someone to plow it while he's away. One of Mitch's clients in Selkirk who knows the guy says he most often goes to Florida. Wherever he spends his winters, by the time he gets back, so much more snow will have fallen that he won't even know it had ever left his property.

Playing chicken with that asswipe was the ultimate rush. Mitch could see the terror in his eyes as he practically blew out his horn before running his precious Benz into the ditch. It didn't explode like Mitch had hoped, but Brent and his babe probably got crushed when it rolled over. He had to admit he felt a little bad for her. But she was a loose end who could have caused problems for him. Collateral damage, as they say. To finish the job, Mitch made sure to throw a match in the gas tank. Watched the car become completely engulfed in flames. *God, that felt good.* It was such a fitting way for that backstabber to go. A traitor of the worst kind. Mitch still can't believe how he allowed himself to get outfoxed so easily. He should never have trusted a professional con man like that. A con man who masterminded a mischievous plot to cheat him out of the national sales manager's job. One that Mitch had rightly earned. And if that wasn't enough, Brent had to rub Mitch's nose in it. The bastard humiliated Mitch. Right in front of everyone. Laughed right in his face. Then, to add further insult, he stole one of Mitch's accounts right from under his nose.

As the car kept burning, Mitch couldn't resist the urge to pull out his phone and record the scene for posterity. He'll have to send the video to Brent's ex at some point. She'll probably burn it to DVD and play it over and over on her big-screen TV. Just like Mitch himself is looking forward to doing some time in the next few days when he gets a bit of a breather.

He only wished he could have filmed the scene in the alley the other night when he took care of Dr. Slant-Eyes. But the lighting was piss-poor. Still, he'd love to be able to relive the moment when he first dragged that box cutter across his face after slitting the bugger's throat. And when, using both of his hands, he drove that thick, long-handled screwdriver into each of his eyes and right through his skull. Over and over. It felt so good. Indescribable, really. There's nothing like the feeling of spilling the blood of someone who had caused you so much suffering. Nothing like it at all. If he had only thought to bring a bottle with him, he'd have saved some of the blood. There was certainly enough of it. Bugger bled like a stuck pig. Then he could put it up on his mantel. He could also send some of it to his widow. Give her something to remember him by. Use it as the centerpiece for some kind of shrine. They do that in Asian cultures. Maybe even light some candles around it.

But she and their kids need not mourn his death. Mitch certainly won't. And neither will his patients. That man truly deserved to die. Even though the cops will call it a murder, in reality Mitch had done the world a favor. He was a real quack. No one should have to get saddled with a so-called doctor like him. He didn't even deserve to be called a doctor. A "doctor" Mitch would never have known if his original family doctor hadn't suddenly retired and dumped him like a hot potato. Of course, Dr. Weinstein made arrangements for most of his other patients. They got in with other doctors in the practice. But not Mitch. Someone who had been seeing him ever since he was a baby was left high and dry. Leaving Mitch to take whoever was available elsewhere in the city. And all he could get was Dr. Cho. A pill-pusher who didn't give two shits about his patients. And cared even less about Mitch. Couldn't get him out of his office fast enough. Which is likely why he's in this ditch right now. If only they had found the mass a little sooner, who knows, they might have been able to do something.

He had originally planned to do the doc the previous night. But he had to wait an extra day. The storm and all. Not to mention the seizure Mitch had earlier in the day. That on the heels of another splitting headache. Which was why he was so much more anxious than normal. He knows his time is running out. He has no time to lose. All day long, he was champing at the bit. Praying for another chance to get the doc. Thankfully, his prayers were answered. And with any luck, he will be able to fully complete his mission before the cancer gets him.

Unfortunately, he'll have to pause that mission for a bit because he has other business to attend to first. An unwanted distraction. But as royally pissed as Mitch is about having to alter the plan, even for an hour, let alone a day, he knows it was inevitable. After all, he was Leah's ex. Plus there was all that shit with the restraining order and the lies everyone concocted about him. So the cops were bound to get around to him sooner or later. He just didn't think it would be so quickly. Those fat cats aren't usually so gung ho. Most often, they're too busy filling their faces at the donut shop. That's why he needs to act now. So he can continue on without any further interruptions. Not that he's at all worried about what they might find with Leah. The police don't have a shred of evidence. They can't have any because there's nothing for them to find. They're just grasping at straws. Straws. That's all they've got. But what he is worried about is the tail they're putting on him. He saw them sitting outside his block the other night as he was sneaking in through a back window in the alley. And if they've got surveillance on him, they're probably tracking him electronically as well. Tapping into his landline and tracking his cell phone. Probably reading his emails too. *Bloody cops have way too much power these days. Bunch of goddamned fascists!* Which was why he picked up a burner phone. He left his regular phone at home. Made sure to leave it on too. So they'll think he hasn't left the building. He also left his own car in the lot. Parked the Impala a couple of blocks away. Different spots each time. Just so nosy neighbors don't start getting too curious about it. All he hopes is that it doesn't get stolen or vandalized. At least not too badly. He can get the tires replaced easily enough if they get slashed. But if the windows get smashed, that could set him back longer. And having to steal another car would be another distraction he doesn't need. It's an old clunker. Something he'd normally be embarrassed to be seen in. But in this case, it's perfect because it doesn't stand out and the owners won't even know it's gone until he's six feet under.

It was a stroke of genius how he had come up with a story on the fly to explain his whereabouts on the night Leah disappeared. Of course, he knew Tommy would go along. Tommy does everything Mitch asks. Peg Leg would even jump off the top of the Richardson Building if Mitch asked. So he shot the prick a text right after hanging up with that so-called detective: "if cops ask, u and I were together Mon night, you know, hanging out like we usually do, thx." And that's exactly what he told her when she called. Like a trained seal. Normally, Mitch has no use for the fucking retard. Guy's got the IQ of a gerbil. A welfare case with a club foot who can't even hold a job salting fries at McDonald's. Always drooling at the mouth. *God, he's pathetic.* The only reason Mitch gives him the time of day is because his father owns a small printing business that's been one of his big clients for years. *Why couldn't they have had a daughter with big bazookas instead?* But Tommy finally made himself useful for once in his miserable life.

Even though he had been able to thoroughly cover his tracks, he was still furious that the bitch was on his trail. He just couldn't get her out of his mind, even when he was butchering Dr. Cho. Just for that, he wanted to really make a scene there. Torch the place. Maybe set off a gas line. Show her who's boss. But that would only attract more attention. And that was the last thing he needed right now.

What he does need to do is regain his focus. So he can take care of business. Only then can he get back to the matter at hand of leaving the world a better place.

And it all starts with a little shut-eye.

Chapter 13

A Loose End
Monday, January 22, 12:18 AM

Mitch tiptoes inside and gently closes the door behind him, being careful not to make a sound. Not even the slightest click as he resets the door handle in place. As much as he wants to finish the job quickly, he cannot afford to let his anxiety get the better of him. He had hoped to have taken care of business long ago and been back in his condo fast asleep. But he had to wait until all the activity had died down. Being so close to the university, no doubt it's the students who are out and about. Getting back after a weekend of partying hard. Mitch knows the life all too well. It wasn't that long ago that he was one of them. He was so shitfaced half the time it's a wonder he was able to pass his exams. This was why he hid in the broom closet for the past hour until he stopped hearing footsteps. A broom closet that was conveniently left unlocked. He'll have to send the super a fruit basket to thank him once he's done. Saved him from having to hide under a stairwell. Because there can't be any witnesses. This is the one job that has to be done right. He knows it will set off a firestorm that will leave him with no margin for error whatsoever. And furthermore, this will likely be his only chance. Now or never. And never wasn't an option.

He takes the backpack off his shoulder and rests it down on the welcome mat, being extra careful not to rattle any of the tools he brought with him. Tools he was shocked he didn't have to use. He thought for sure this was the one unit where the deadbolt would be on. All he had to do was pick the flimsy lock. *Christ, all I needed was a bobby pin!*

He was also shocked by how easily he found the address. He just had to look in the phone book. Let your fingers do the walking. Despite all the crazies and nuts out there, especially in this town, people keep making it so goddamned easy. He even got the suite number. And as luck would have it, a neighboring unit was for sale. The agent was kind enough to post a video as part of the listing showing all around the unit. Which are all pretty much identical in these blocks. So he knew he would hardly need the night vision goggles once he got inside. Security in the block had the potential to be a bit of a problem though. He had some ideas for how to get inside. He could try the usual stunt of posing as a repairman or a city worker.

Just as he had done to get into the Kleins' house. And it probably would have worked. He could also have dressed up as a courier driver, rung a unit and said he had a parcel for them. People wouldn't think twice before buzzing you in. To make it look authentic, he could have stolen another delivery truck. Which sure wouldn't have been difficult. Those guys always leave the keys in the ignition and the motor running. Can't possibly make it any easier. Another idea he had was to dress up as a clown. Wait at the door until someone comes by. Then tell them that it's a surprise singing telegram or something. Anyone would surely let him in with no problem. But wearing such a gaudy outfit might attract attention. No, he needed to come and go and have no one know he was ever there. So he almost had to laugh when someone held the door open for him. Didn't even ask if he lived there. *What the hell's the point of having security in the building when people will just let you in? Friendly Manitoba to the rescue.*

After slipping off his boots, he makes his way into the kitchen. There are no lights on, but he can see perfectly well without the goggles, as the streetlights on Pembina Highway shine through the picture window. *Thanks for leaving the drapes open.* He can see the marble backsplash. The quartz countertop. And the crystal chandelier. *Must be doing pretty well.* Whole lot better than him, that's for sure. He can barely afford to keep the lights on in his little hovel. One that he shares with a few dozen roaches. Roaches that would love the half-eaten salad that's in the plastic takeout container on the counter. Even he'd go for it right about now. He's absolutely famished. But first, he needs to take care of business. Then he can help himself. He does, however, help himself to the ice pick lying on the counter. He had brought a knife with him. A damned good one too. Military grade. It would do the job quite well. But that pick will do much better. So he transfers the knife from his right to his left pocket and stuffs the pick in his right.

With both weapons in tow, he scurries along the slick laminate flooring in his stocking feet, focused on the sliding barn door by the window separating the living room from the bedroom. But in his haste, he bumps into the corner of the glass table in front of the sofa, rattling a cup sitting next to the remote control for the big-screen TV. *Shit!* He freezes. There is dead silence. He waits. And waits. Still no sound. A half minute later, he begins breathing again when he hears muffled snoring coming from the other side of the wall. *Still sound asleep. Thank Christ!* After counting his lucky stars, he moves up alongside the barn door. A door that was conveniently left open. *How nice!* He takes a couple of baby steps and slowly peers around the corner. His target is perfectly still. Under the covers and facing away from him. All he can see is the blond hair.

He knows this is the time to act. So after feeling the handle of the ice pick inside the right pocket of his black jacket to make sure it's still there, he tiptoes around the corner. He quickly sizes up the small bedroom. There's more room for him over on the left side of the bed. But that's where his target is facing. No, he must approach with stealth. So he sneaks sideways along the narrow strip between the floor-to-ceiling curtain covering the window and the right side of the bed. With his target remaining perfectly still in the middle of the queen-size bed, he leaps up onto the mattress. With both hands, he twists her head down and holds it there. Then before she can make a sound, he takes his right hand off the mop of blond hair and reaches into his pocket for the pick. He pulls it out, raises it high above his head and drives it down with all his might. Cracking her thick skull and plunging it deep into her brain. She has gone limp. He removes his left hand from the back of her head. He no longer has to hold her down. She's not going anywhere. Except downstairs. But that sound of her skull cracking has set him aflame. His pulse is racing. The endorphins are flowing like a raging river. So he pulls out the pick and drives it in again. And again. And again. Then into her neck. Over and over. Splattering blood. On his gloves. On his arm. All over the pillows. The headboard. And the wall. Only when he has completely severed the spinal column does he stop. He cannot leave anything to chance. She cannot be left a vegetable. There must be closure.

Physically exhausted, his forearm speckled with her blood, he wipes some of the sweat off his brow, streaking the blood across his forehead and into his eyebrows. He is still breathing heavily. The sweat and diluted blood continue to drip over his eyes. But slowly, he begins to calm down. He takes long and slow breaths. Then he climbs off the bed and gets back on his feet, leaving the pick right by her head. He stops to admire his work. His target is still lying facedown, covered in a pool of her own blood. As his heart rate starts slowing, he wonders if he should turn her around. Have her faceup when her friends or family come to check on her. Assuming the miserable bitch even has anyone in her life who cares about her. And so he can see her face. Just once. But he thinks better of it. Best to just leave her that way. Maybe once they're done with the autopsy, they'll put her in the ground that way too. Or better yet, incinerate her. Leave nothing but ashes. Ashes to dump in the Red with the rest of the sewage.

As he digs out his phone to snap a shot of the scene, he realizes this wasn't just a job. It was personal. Just like all the others. She must have had it in for him right from the beginning. She wanted to get him. *Needed* to get him. And she wasn't going to rest until she had stopped him dead in his tracks. He knows that now. But he was able to turn the tables. Now she's the one who's stopped. Cold. And she won't be missed, that's for sure. No doubt, she'll soon be frolicking in the bowels of Satan's kingdom where she belongs. He only wishes he had been able to make her suffer first. She didn't deserve to go quietly. He wishes he could have really made a statement with her. He thought about stripping her naked and hanging her upside down from the ceiling right in front of the window. Then slice her open and rip her heart out. Like on *Predator*. Or cut her head off with a machete. Like the guy on the Greyhound bus did. Then mount her head on a pole and stick it in the ground at the bus stop across the street. But this one needed to be clean.

And it had been clean. Smooth. By the numbers. Exactly the way he planned it. This'll sure get 'em off his back. Give them bigger fish to fry. Things had gone so smoothly, in fact, that, looking at his watch, he sees he has a little extra time on his hands. Time to fix himself a quick meal in the kitchen before he tidies up some other loose ends on his way out. He just hopes there's something good in the fridge. *It would be a shame for it to go to waste.*

Because she sure won't be needing it anymore.

Chapter 14

Bad News
Monday, January 22, 8:52 AM

As the morning meeting drags on, Sierra notices Norm reach across the table to open up the second box of donuts. Instantly, she turns up her nose and looks away. She can't bear to look at another donut, let alone eat one. The two she had at Friday's meeting were enough to last her for, like, the rest of the year. Maybe even her entire life. They settled in her stomach like a couple of bricks. And blew up like balloons. They probably made her look six months pregnant. Hopefully, underneath that big parka, no one noticed. She'd have died of embarrassment if anyone saw that baby bump.

Looking up at the clock, she is only shocked that it has taken Norm so long to dig into the second box. Normally, he'd be well into it long before now. She can only surmise that he's not fully awake yet. He probably spent most of the weekend drowning his sorrows in a bottle at the Riverside. Talking about the good old days with the rest of his buddies. Truth of the matter is that she couldn't care less how he spends his weekends. But Sierra doesn't need to hear all the boring details at the meeting. And at her desk. And during the chief's presentation. And at the weekly departmental meeting. And during the sensitivity training sessions. And during the Aboriginal cultural awareness training. And at the union briefings. If we wanted to hear about the latest hockey news or who can belch the loudest, she could go to the Riverside and find out for herself. That is, assuming she'd be caught dead in a sleazy place like that.

It was a much different weekend for Sierra, who spent the time pampering herself at the nearby Four Points hotel. Victoria was becoming just too much to deal with. So instead of getting into another shouting match or throwing more things around, she packed an overnight bag and left. No doubt to the silent cheering of their neighbors. Things had been getting a little unruly lately, Sierra had to admit. But it wasn't *that* bad. There was no reason to make a formal complaint to the homeowners' association about it. Stuff happens. They've certainly heard their fair share of noise from others in the block. Like the Halloween party that went on till three in the morning. Or the New Year's Eve bash that the whole building could hear. Nobody said anything about that. But everyone flies off the handle the moment the two of them have a spat.

For sure, there were no wild parties for Sierra this weekend. Just lots of rest and relaxation. Alone. Hardly saw a soul after she checked in. The Jacuzzi in her room was wonderful. So relaxing. Hung out a bit in the sauna. Where she nearly got electrocuted when some guy came charging in, ready to throw a bucket of water on the coals without reading the big sign saying it was an electric sauna. Thank goodness that maintenance guy stopped him. "You'll light up like a Christmas tree," he said. The best part of the whole weekend, however, was that she didn't hear a thing from Victoria. Not a word. Not even a tiny peep. And damned if Sierra was going to call her. If Victoria wants to play the silent treatment game, she's in for quite a battle.

The time away allowed Sierra to focus on their relationship. And what's left of it isn't pretty. In fact, it's gotten downright ugly. She kept hoping Victoria would come around. If for no other reason than it would save her the trouble of moving out. Not to mention finding a place. Especially in winter. A hell of a time to move. Wind chill was −45 last night. Makes her wonder why she, or anyone else for that matter, still lives here. But Victoria hasn't come around. And isn't bloody well likely to do so. It's getting to the point that one of them is going to end up killing the other. So Sierra needs to move on. Once she gets her own space and settles down, then she can figure out where she's going. Find someone new. Or just play the field. Experiment a little. Get a little kinky. Part of her has always wanted to be in a threesome with another woman and a man. Maybe a married couple. That'd be interesting. See where it goes. And above all else, have some fun.

While Norm stuffs his face with another donut, the rest of the group keeps talking about that horrible accident north of the city over the weekend. On Saturday morning, an SUV overturned out in the middle of nowhere and caught fire. Burned to a crisp. Just like the remains of the two bodies they found inside. From running the possible matches with what's left of the car, they're pretty sure it's a guy who lives nearby in a big three-acre mansion along the river in East St. Paul. But they can't release any details until the bodies have been positively identified. One of our investigators who was called out to assist the Mounties said they'll need to check dental records. Not much else to go on. Hell of a way to go. Mounties say the guy probably just lost control on the icy highway. Likely another case of driving too fast for conditions. Something Sierra has been guilty of herself on occasion.

Sierra led off the meeting with an update on her case. Not that there was much new to report. No new leads and still no sign of the missing woman. She's still working angles on her husband and her ex. See if something comes up. But nothing has. At least so far. Especially with the ex. Had him under surveillance all weekend, but the guys said he didn't leave his block. Not even once. So Andrea decided to call them off. Can't afford to waste any more resources pursuing a wild goose chase, she said. With no sign of the woman, it won't be long before the brass will officially list the case a homicide. Which it probably is. Leah might have even been dead before Sierra ever got the call to go out to the house. And even if she was still alive, she's probably long gone by now. They can still hope, of course. Sierra tried to sound optimistic when Dr. Klein called on Friday asking for an update. The kids want to know when their mommy is coming home. But the odds of her suddenly showing up at their front door sure aren't looking very good. All they can hope for right now is to find a body. Give the family some closure at least. The uncertainty is probably killing them more than anything.

Not that the homicide designation changes anything though. Except for the media. They'll be all over it once it's announced. Likely at the Wednesday press conference. Probably generate more headlines. But as much as the WPS hates the inevitable Monday morning quarterbacking and the public scrutiny it brings, Sierra couldn't help but think something good could potentially come out of it. Not that she would dare say such a thing to Andrea, of course. Maybe another lead could come their way. Perhaps someone saw something and just didn't think to call it in. You never know. They need all the help they can get right now.

The only other hot case they talked about at the meeting was the one involving the doctor who was hacked up in the alley behind his own clinic. But like her case, there wasn't much new to report. Ken said there was no surveillance footage and though there were plenty of prints around the place, they didn't necessarily point to the perp or perps. After all, plenty of people came and went, as it was a busy place with the doctor's office and pharmacy being right across from each other. There were also tenants on the second floor. One was an accountant's office and the other was a software development company. They make games and such. Virtual reality. Neither office was touched. Even though the accountant admitted to having several thousand dollars in his safe. Ken said the autopsy was scheduled for this week and he wants to be there for it. He's hoping for some more insight. Not just the type of weapon used, but he's hoping to be able to recreate how the actual murder was committed. Was he ambushed? Which might indicate a planned killing. Or was he just in the wrong place at the wrong time? Andrea still thinks it's the latter and that he's wasting his time. She wants Ken to look into the big-time pusher the vice unit just picked up. It fits his M.O., she said. Aggravated robbery. Assault with a deadly weapon. That in addition to his other drug charges. He's got ties to gangs. But Ken's still focused on the doctor. He wants to go through his records and see if there's someone who might have a beef with him. But that could take forever, Andrea said. And tie up resources we don't have. She's still letting Ken roll with his theory. For now. But if nothing else comes up by the end of the week, she said he's going to have to put it on ice.

Andrea also couldn't stop gushing about how productive the special Friday afternoon interdepartmental meeting was. Yet as she spoke, Sierra could see eyes rolling around the table. Those old-school dinosaurs just don't get it. Or don't want to get it. It still amazes Sierra how pigheaded some people can be. But Andrea was right. Those team-building exercises were invaluable. She would never have guessed that Ken dabbles in writing poetry. Or that Corazon is a big fan of action movies like *The Terminator*. Plus it gave them a chance to meet people from other departments they don't normally interact with. You can't put a price on what it means to forge those relationships. Especially over the long haul. As the group leaders said, there's no limit to what we can accomplish when we work together as a cohesive unit. It was such a fitting way to wrap up the day. They were absolutely fabulous. Despite all the skepticism in the room, it was worth every penny to fly them in from Toronto. It's no wonder they have such a thriving consulting business helping organizations learn new processes to help them navigate through challenging times. Sierra only wished she could have joined Andrea and the chief as they took the consultants for dinner afterward before they caught their flight back home.

Just as the chatter about the accident begins to die down, Andrea's phone goes off. Sierra has always liked her ringtone. The gentle strumming of a guitar. One of these days, she wants to ask Andrea where she got it from. She's been Googling it and can't seem to find it anywhere. It takes her back to when she learned to play the guitar in elementary school. Her music teacher was a real hoot. All the kids loved her. She was one of the most memorable teachers she ever had. But just as Sierra gets lost in her past, she turns toward Andrea and notices a sudden look of concern on her face as she studies the call display. "I have to take this," she says as she presses the talk button. The normally cheery expression on her face quickly evaporates as she mostly listens to the person on the other end of the line. "Yes. . . . I understand. . . . Are you sure? . . . Where are you? . . . Yes, she's right here. . . . All right. . . . We'll be there right away."

Andrea hangs up, then glances over at Sierra with a gray, expressionless look on her face. "Meeting adjourned," she says sullenly. Sierra joins the others in getting up to leave. "Not you," Andrea says. So she falls back into her chair while the others file out. Corazon is the last to leave. She asks Andrea if she wants her to close the door. "Yes, please," Andrea says.

Once the door closes, the silence in the room becomes oppressive. Sierra is dying to know what's going on. *Am I in trouble?* She doesn't have long to wait. Andrea turns to face her. "I'm afraid I have some bad news," she says. Stiff as a board, Sierra listens as Andrea spells it out. Once Andrea has finished speaking, she sits there silently processing the information, unable to believe what she just heard. Then her eyes begin to well up.

And she begins to cry.

Chapter 15

In Cold Blood
Monday, January 22, 4:31 PM

Sierra is shivering in the back of a cruiser parked in front of her block. The musty and smelly blanket draped around her shoulders offers little protection from the bitter cold. *They could at least leave the car running with the heater on.* She is still in a state of shock. She can't believe Victoria is dead. Murdered in cold blood. *Who would want to kill her? And so brutally.* Stabbed with an ice pick through her skull is what they told her. As she was sleeping in the bed they shared. A bed Sierra might have been in if she hadn't gone to the hotel. She can't bear to think about it. It's just so awful. It doesn't seem real. Things like this are only supposed to happen in horror movies. Not in real life. It's like a bad dream. A nightmare.

Tightly gripping both her hands around the hot coffee Andrea just brought her, Sierra aimlessly gazes out the frosted-up window toward Pembina Highway. It should be jam-packed with commuters at this hour. People who had a long day at the office and are looking forward to a hot meal and a good night's sleep before gearing up to do the same thing again tomorrow. But tonight, they have to find another way home. The yellow tape squad has cordoned off Pembina in both directions. She's never understood why they keep getting away with being so bloody obnoxious. Shutting down the city's busiest traffic artery for absolutely no reason. Victoria was killed in their condo, not on the street. But right now, she doesn't give a shit. At least it's keeping the television cameras at bay. She can see the bright lights of their trucks parked at the strip mall across the street. Providing up-to-the-minute coverage of the horrific murder that has sent shock waves across the city. It's on all the newscasts and probably will be on the front page of all the papers tomorrow. The inside scoop on how Winnipeg's answer to Marilyn Monroe met her untimely death. It makes her want to crawl under a rock somewhere. She doesn't want to be the news.

She shades her eyes just as one of those news trucks shines their spotlight in her direction. Probably going live with another update. But then she hears tapping on the ice-covered window. Probably Andrea, she thinks. And as the door opens on the driver's side, her suspicion is confirmed. Andrea leans in and holds out a paper bag. Sierra reaches and takes it. Inside are probably a couple of donuts. Whatever they are, she doesn't want them. Even if she were hungry. So she forces a smile and hands the bag back to Andrea. "Thanks," Sierra mumbles. *Give them to someone else. With all these cops around, they sure won't go to waste.* Andrea asks if Sierra would like to talk. *She's been a real doll in all of this.* But Sierra's in no mood for any more chatter. She just wants to be alone. And to have this whole nasty business go away. But it won't be going away for a hell of a long while.

For starters, Sierra has been put on administrative leave, effective immediately. Someone else, probably Corazon, is going to have to try to track down that missing woman. And her killer. *Good luck.* It's standard procedure, Andrea says. And not just for compassionate reasons. Because it sure sounds like the Independent Investigations Unit is trying to frame her with the murder. The group that gets called in any time there's the possibility of police involvement. Sure, the two of them were having problems. The neighbors can sure attest to that, if they haven't already. They can probably give full transcripts of everything they said. But just because Sierra said that one of them might end up killing the other, she didn't mean it literally. Even if Victoria was cavorting around with someone else. Which she probably was, since there was no sign of forced entry. It would have been impossible to get in unless Victoria let them in. Sierra is the only other person with a key. And it's a secured block. They've got a deadbolt on the door with a good lock. So unless Spider-Man swooped in onto the balcony and jimmied the latch on the sliding glass door, that's the only possible explanation. So they found Sierra's prints on the ice pick. Well, duh, she just used it a couple of days ago. Victoria's prints are probably on it too.

Right from the start, Sierra told Andrea she had nothing to do with Victoria's murder. She knows Andrea believes her. But as Andrea said, her opinion doesn't matter. It's completely out of her hands. The IIU is running the show. And they've got one of their top assholes in charge of the investigation. Al Hunt. A 30-year vet of the force who's been in IIU for a few years. One of those old-school cops with a beer belly who always has a cigarette hanging out of his mouth and a chip on his shoulder. Sierra heard about him from a fellow recruit right after she graduated from the Academy. "I had to earn my way on the force, young lady," he said to her. "They didn't lower the standards for me, why the hell should they for you? And don't get me started on the faggots. Shouldn't even let 'em on the goddamned force at all, let alone giving them special privileges." Needless to say, as soon as he got the job, the chief made it his top priority to get rid of bigots like him. But he couldn't fire him. The union would have fought it tooth and nail. So he kicked him over to IIU. Internal Affairs, as it was known at the time. And now that brute has Sierra in his crosshairs. Ready to ship her off to jail. Probably already getting a cell ready at the new women's facility out in Headingley. All for a murder she didn't commit. "It doesn't look good for her," he told Andrea. "She might want to think about finding a good lawyer. And tell her not to leave town."

Leaving town is something Sierra would love to do. Not because she's guilty. But just to get away from everything. From everyone. Not to mention the cold. Go frolic on a beach somewhere. Somewhere warm. But that's not an option right now. She doesn't even know where she'll be spending the night. Probably back at the hotel. It's her best option right now. Perhaps her only option. She can't bear to move back in with her parents. She just wants to be alone. And she sure won't be able to get into her condo for a while. Not that she really wants to go back there. Ever. Except to get her things. She'd love to put it on the market right now. Take the money and run. But who'd want to buy a condo the Grim Reaper hacked someone up in? *You too can own your own personal house of horrors. Yeah, that'll make great copy for the listing.*

Sadly, she will probably have to hire a lawyer. Not that she wants to. But even she has to admit there *is* incriminating evidence. People have been sent up the river for far less. Especially in Manitoba. She's heard about enough cases and even seen a couple herself. The problem is she doesn't even know where to start looking for a lawyer. The only one who comes to mind is Marty Morgenstern. The guy who defended the cop who killed that woman while driving drunk. He could get anyone off. Even the likes of Ted Bundy. Sounds like a real sleazeball though. She'll ask around. See if she can do better. The Rainbow Resource Center might be a good place to start. They'd be able to put her in touch with a like-minded progressive. The last thing she needs is to put her life in the hands of another member of the old boys' club. She needs someone who will actually take her case seriously. And care about *her.*

But the question still remains as to who killed Victoria. *What sort of monster would do this?* Sure, the two of them had their problems, but Victoria was still a lovely person. She didn't deserve this. Whoever the sicko is, Sierra is going to have to find him. Or her. Because if she doesn't, she might very well end up taking the ride for it. And she's probably going to have to handle this daunting task all on her own. She knows she won't be able to expect any help from the likes of Al Hunt or anyone else at IIU. For all she knows, he'll probably be meeting with the Crown prosecutor first thing tomorrow morning to get an indictment on a first-degree murder charge.

Where to start is making her head spin. It literally could be anybody. Victoria knew everyone in town, it seems. And everyone knew her. Maybe it was some lovestruck fan. *Who knows?* But even though Sierra will have plenty of time on her hands, she will have to get started right away. There isn't a minute to lose. Her freedom is on the line.

But that will have to wait until tomorrow. She is completely wiped out. The day has taken an incredible toll on her. She barely has enough energy to hold on to the cup of coffee in her hands. Right now, she just wants to lie down, close her eyes and go to sleep.

And hope that by the time she wakes up, this will all have been just a bad dream.

Chapter 16

Hit and Run
Tuesday, January 23, 2:12 AM

Having just put up his hood and zipped up his parka, Winston Grayson digs out the keys from his pocket as he steps outside. Before ending his shift at the convenience store, he has to lock the front door, then secure the metal gate. Even the bullet-proof glass isn't enough to stop the criminal element in this part of town. But before turning his back, he carefully looks around, making sure no one is lurking nearby. He knows he can't afford to get careless. Not for a second. There's a stabbing or shooting nearly every night around here. One night three weeks ago, someone came around the corner when he was locking up and tried to jump him. Luckily, he was able to overpower the scumbag, who got spooked and ran off. Winston didn't even bother calling the cops afterward. Unless a gallon or two of blood has been spilled, it doesn't register on their radar. They've got bigger fish to fry. No harm, no foul.

It wasn't always like this for Winston. He'd had a good job. He had just gotten a promotion, in fact, along with a nice raise. His personal life was great too. He lived in a nice apartment in a hip neighborhood. Lots of bars and restaurants around. He had a steady girlfriend and the two of them were talking about buying a condo together. Settle down, get married and eventually start a family. Life was good. But then, out of the blue, everything fell apart. He made a mistake. Not even a mistake, a bit of poor judgment. He thought nothing of it. It goes on all the time. He's sure every single one of his colleagues have even done it at least once one time or another. All he was trying to do was help a buddy and a good customer. You scratch my back and I'll scratch yours. And there'd be no way anyone would find out, he thought. He still can't figure out how they could have discovered it was him. But in any event, after the second round of questioning by the detectives, he did the right thing and came clean. Admitted he was wrong. Apologized. He even testified in court. What more was he supposed to do? How could he possibly have known how things were going to end up? He's not the Amazing Kreskin, for Christ's sake. But that still didn't matter. They still cut him loose. Fine. There's other fish in the sea, he thought. But that was just the beginning. As he found out, Winnipeg, at its core, is still a small town. Word gets around. People talk. He was damaged goods. No one would hire him. No one. He couldn't even get a job working the graveyard shift stocking shelves at the Superstore.

As he blew through his meager savings, he lost his apartment because he couldn't afford the rent anymore. He had hoped to move in with his girlfriend, but she dumped him like a hot potato as soon as the balance in his bank account began to bottom out. It's not you, it's me, she said. She couldn't even have come up with something more original. And then she promptly took up with some hotshot who drives a black Beemer. *Guess that Beemer was a little more "her."* So he had to bounce around from friend to friend, finding a place to crash wherever he could. One day here. Two days there. He felt lucky if he got a full week at the same place. It was only after finally finding work at the convenience store that he was able to afford that rooming house nearby. One that he shares with a bunch of gangbangers and drug dealers, not to mention all the rats and cockroaches.

With the streetlight at the other end of the block providing a little illumination, Winston sees that the coast is clear. No creature is stirring. Not even a mouse. So he turns his back to lock the doors, then turns around and gives a cursory glance in both directions before darting across the street. He hardly has to bother checking, since there's almost never anyone on the roads at this hour. Walking home after work, all he usually hears are the sirens from ambulances or fire trucks. But still, he knows it's better to be safe than sorry. After crossing all four lanes and scaling the three-foot-high windrow of snow on the opposite side, he turns the corner past the low-cost housing block directly across from the store and sets off down Alexander Avenue to begin his walk home. Normally, it takes him a little over 10 minutes. But as he gets bogged down in the nearly knee-deep snow, he realizes it's going to take a bit longer.

Trudging through the snow drifts leaves Winston exhausted by the time he gets to the three-way stop at Ellen Street, where he spots a car approaching, the first one he's seen since leaving the store. He thinks about waiting for him to go, but he's tired. He wants to get home. He doesn't want to wait any longer and the car is still a couple of blocks away from the stop sign. He figures it's safe, even in virtual darkness, so he steps off the curb, treading gingerly, an inch at a time on the smooth, slippery ice. Trying desperately to keep his balance and not fall, he fails to notice that the car is not slowing down, but rather, picking up speed. It is not until Winston is smack-dab in the middle of the street that he realizes the driver has no intention of stopping. *Dude, you've got a stop sign!*

He knows he's in a hell of a spot. If the driver doesn't see the stop sign, he probably doesn't see him either. So he needs to get the hell out of his way. Otherwise, he'll get flattened like a pancake. So he decides to backtrack as fast as he can without falling flat on his ass. With any luck, he'll at least be able to get out of the guy's lane. He manages a couple of baby steps, then he hears the car's engine roar. The driver has floored it. He turns and sees the faint glimmer of the grill headed right for him. *What the hell are you doing, asshole?!* He thinks to put up his arms to try to wave. Anything to get the driver's attention. But he is too late. The car plows right into him. He goes flying over the hood. He can do nothing to prevent his head from smashing into the windshield. He blacks out instantly as he rolls off the side of the car and onto a snowbank.

When he comes to a few seconds later, he is lying flat on his back, staring up at the streetlight high above him. His first sensation is the taste of warm blood. He wants to cough but can't summon up the energy. He is weak. He can barely move. And he is in a fog. He has no idea where he is, what has happened or even what day it is. All he knows is that something pretty bad happened. He just hopes help is on the way. And soon.

He hears the roar of an engine. It's got to be the paramedics, he thinks. *They're here to take me to the Health Sciences Center.* Thank God, he mutters. Because he's in a hell of a lot of pain. It hurts all over. The sound gets louder. Then he feels a sudden impact against his rib cage. Probably the back wheel of the ambulance, he thinks. *Christ, what's going on? You're here to help me, aren't you?* He feels his ribs begin to buckle as the wheel keeps pressing against his midsection. In desperation, he bangs on the side of the vehicle, but it continues to slowly crush him. He feels like a grape caught in a juice squeezer. His breaths become increasingly short. Soon he can draw no more air into his flattened lungs.

Then he passes out.

Chapter 17

Back to Work
Friday, January 26, 7:31 AM

It has been a rough couple of days for Mitch. But after resting up as best he could following his radiation treatment, he's once again ready to go. The nukes certainly did a hell of a number on him. He could barely find enough energy to get out of bed. They said it would improve his quality of life, at least for the little time he has left. That's why his oncologist kept bugging him to go. So he finally did. At least it would shut the bugger up. But it sure as hell doesn't feel like much of an improvement. It was probably Dr. Hussain's idea. That son of a bitch. Delivering a death sentence didn't make him happy enough. Now he has to make Mitch suffer even more before he kicks the bucket. Really do a happy dance. That's what they must teach them in med school. Stick it to your patients and dance on their graves. Well, at least Mitch knows now. He won't give that asshole any more satisfaction. When checking out, the receptionist insisted on making another appointment, but there's no way he's going back. Truth is, he should have known it was a trick right from the get-go. Doctors aren't normally so insistent that you actually go for these things. If you go, great. If you don't, well, that's up to you. They don't give a shit either way. No skin off their nose. But he can't waste any more time kicking himself. Time is the most valuable commodity he has. And he's rapidly running short of it.

Having all that time on the shelf at least afforded him the chance to get the Impala fixed up. His guy at the body shop left him a message last night saying it was ready. Good as new, he said. Patched up the grill. New windshield. Pounded out the dents. Only a few scratches. Buffed them out as best he could. Even got it fully detailed. This morning, as soon as he gets dressed and fixes himself something to eat, Mitch will take the bus out there and pick it up. Russ is a great guy. Quick and efficient. But most importantly, he doesn't ask questions. As long as you've got the cash, it doesn't matter. Everyone knows about his chop shop. Even the cops. They've raided it a couple of times. But they never find anything. And Russ never rats out anyone. But damn, Mitch wishes his shop wasn't so far out. If only it were on a major bus route, not way out in the sticks. With the wait between buses, not to mention the 15-minute walk, even if everything goes well, it will take him about two hours to get out there. Assuming that poky little feeder route actually shows up. You can take nothing for granted with Winnipeg Transit. About all you can count on is that the more you need the bus in this town, the less likely it is to show up. Mitch can only keep his fingers crossed that he won't need to take any more buses.

Mitch knows Russ is discreet, but one thing that might have raised his dander was the blood. Dealing in organized auto theft rings is one thing. Murder is quite another. So just to be on the safe side, Mitch had to be certain to clean up the mess before taking it in. The boy's guts splattered all over the undercarriage. It was especially tough to get it out of the treads in the tires. A simple car wash wasn't going to get it done. He had to get down on his hands and knees and scrub. And he had to do it right away before it froze. Son of a bitch deserved to die just for that alone. If only Mitch had been able to get him with the first blow. Winston was resilient though. That big brute sure didn't go down easy. Forced Mitch to take a second run at him. Even then, Mitch had to get out and take his pulse afterward. He had to be sure. Only then did he grab his wallet before taking off. Not that he figured Winston had a lot of cash on him. But whatever he had Mitch was more than entitled to after all Winston had done to him. He had double-crossed him. It had to have been Winston's plan right from the start. And Mitch fell for it. Like a real sucker. He trusted Winston. They were cool. Then suddenly the cops show up at Mitch's door. He knew right away who ratted him out. Winston. Guy must have sung like a canary to the cops. Just like he did in the courtroom. No way those charges would have stuck without Winston's testimony. Even in that kangaroo court.

He was surprised that Winston made it so easy for him. Over the last few days, Mitch could have set his watch by the guy. Never seen anyone more of a slave to routine before. He thought Winston was more cagey than that. Because he had to know Mitch would be coming for him sooner or later. That's what happens to snitches. It was why Mitch wanted to do it face to face. Right in the store. There was no bullet-resistant barrier. Not even any security cameras that he noticed. All he would need to have done was walk in there and go through the usual stick-em-up routine. Then after grabbing a wad of bills out of the cash drawer, he could drive the knife into his gut. Look him right between the eyes as Mitch drained the lifeblood out of him. Then slash the lowlife to pieces. Bone him like a fish. Spill his blood all over the floor. Paint the whole damn store red. But as tempting as it was, in this case, discretion was the better part of valor. Not that he thought the cops would figure it out any time soon, but the last thing he needed was another murder investigation potentially headed his way. So he had to do it this way. He knew the cops wouldn't bat an eye. In fact, Mitch was surprised it even made the news. Another pedestrian killed in a hit and run. *Yawn!* Happens all the time in Winnipeg. The only reason they even mentioned it in the press conference and in the news release is because they still haven't positively identified him yet. And they probably won't for a while. Maybe Mitch should have sent them his driver's license instead of just tossing it along with the rest of his wallet into that dumpster at the other end of town. Of course, they say they're appealing to the public for information. Like people in that area are actually going to say anything. They know better than to blab to the cops even if they did see something. They're not snitches. They know better than to be like Winston.

The previous night was very different. No discretion there. Mitch needed to make a splash. And boy, did he ever. The whole town is talking about it. About him. Everything went so much better than he could possibly have imagined. Naturally, he's still disappointed he missed out on getting the detective. He wanted her so badly he could taste it. He wanted to feel her blood on his hands. Feel her dying in his arms. How could he possibly have known she was a dyke? Shacking up with Vickie C of all people. When he heard the news reports, he was sick to his stomach. She was one hell of a hot babe. Met her at a party once. She could sure knock them back. And she did more coke that night than he did. She was living the high life, that's for sure. And now she's gone. Oh well. More collateral damage. But he sure won't have anything more to worry about as far as the detective is concerned. That's what he really needed out of all this. Better yet, the cops are going off in all the wrong directions. They're running around like chickens with their heads cut off. And Leah and Dr. Slant-Eyes are already yesterday's news. Won't be long before they'll be completely off the radar. Who knows, maybe they'll put all the pieces together someday. But even if they do, it won't happen until long after Mitch is dead and buried. More than likely, it will end up as one of those unsolved mysteries. Books will be written about it. Maybe he'll be the posthumous star of a TV series. Watching those fools fumble about, all he can do is laugh.

For now, it's back to work for Mitch. Once he picks off some low-lying fruit, he'll finally be able to focus on the grand prize.

Revenge is a dish best served cold.

Chapter 18

Paisley
Friday, January 26, 9:18 PM

Just as it had tonight, meetings with Green New Deal Winnipeg always make Paisley Frankel feel so wonderful inside. They leave her with so much warmth in her heart that she feels like she's in Bora Bora, where she and her husband honeymooned, even though the wind chill will be going down to −44 this evening. She loves spearheading grassroots organizations that champion progressive topics like the climate emergency that threatens the planet with extinction. It's exactly why she got into politics. Yet as a second-term city councilor, there's only so much she can do. Which is why so many have encouraged her to run for mayor in the next municipal election. There are far too many buffoons at City Hall who are still stuck in the Stone Age, married to their outdated ideals. Not the least of which is Mayor McShane. For the life of her, she couldn't understand why he was so opposed to redirecting funds from the road repair budget to putting up flower baskets at the corner of Stafford and Academy. He just kept harping on how bad the roads are. Potholes, potholes, potholes. Went on and on like a broken record. Paisley tried to stress that people don't come to Winnipeg to look at the roads, but he just wouldn't listen to reason. Then he fought her tooth and nail on the tree bylaw she introduced. Winnipeg's tree canopy is vitally important and must be protected at all costs. No one in the city should be allowed to cut down a tree willy-nilly. No one. Yet all he did was moan and groan, spewing a bunch of mumbo jumbo about how private property rights must be respected. What about *our* rights? What about the right of future generations to inherit a sustainable planet? He couldn't even make up his mind about safe injection sites despite the glaring need. The opioid crisis has claimed far too many lives. People are crying out for help. And they need it *now*. Yet all he could say was that he needed more time to think it over. *What's there to think over? All the experts agree that the harm reduction approach is the only viable solution.*

As tempting as taking on Mayor McShane would be, however, there is so much more she could accomplish at the provincial level. And that's why she's got her eye on the vacant leadership of the NDP. She hasn't made up her mind yet, but all her friends say she would be a shoo-in if she were to declare her candidacy. She knows she has tons of support within the party membership as well as the union leadership. She'd hardly need the new antidiscrimination measures giving preference to women and people of color to put her over the top. And with her at the helm, there's no question the party's popularity would skyrocket once again and put her in a position to make history and become Manitoba's first female premier when the next provincial election rolls around in a couple of years' time.

One of the first things she would do after taking office would be to have the stone pillars in front of the Legislative Building painted in rainbow colors. Not only would it spruce up that hideous old façade, but it would make such a bold statement showing off Manitoba as the most inclusive and welcoming province in Canada for members of the sexually diverse and gender-fluid communities. So many cities have rainbow crosswalks, but something like that could have a much bigger impact. Time and again, she's tried to convince her fellow councilors to do up City Hall the same way. In fact, it was one of the first things she proposed right after being elected. Yet there was so much pushback. It was incredible. More shocking was all the hateful venom and vitriol directed her way on social media. But she remains determined not to back down in the face of homophobia, and she was proud to lead the charge for the rainbow-colored curbs at the corner of Portage and Main, the most famous intersection in the country. It's not much, but it's a start.

With that out of the way, she could begin to tackle some of the other items on her agenda. Of course, the health care system would need a major overhaul. Union leaders have rightly been up in arms for years about how overworked health care administrators have been and how far their compensation has been lagging behind. Yet this current government can't get its head out of its ass. Doctors and nurses need all the administrative support they can get, and the regional health authority system, which provides an additional layer of oversight at the local level, is vital. The notion that the system is drowning in bureaucracy is preposterous. Then the government goes on and on about restraint and spending only within our means, parroting that ridiculous populist drivel. Manitoba just simply cannot afford austerity. Can't be done. And if they're so worried about money, why not just use carbon tax revenues to fund pay increases? There's plenty of it to go around and it's a perfectly logical solution. But instead of praising the visionary union leader who proposed it, the health minister actually mocked him. Even called the union greedy. Well, you just can't fix stupid. Anyone who thinks those idiots shouldn't be booted out of office shouldn't be allowed to vote. Plain and simple. Just take all the conservatives off the list of electors with one big clean sweep. And while they're at it, make votes from women and people of color count double. It only makes sense given how underrepresented they are in elected office.

Then there's the justice system. For years, one of Paisley's biggest pet peeves has been the shocking number of Aboriginals unfairly locked up behind bars. Who can blame them for lashing out? In addition to the systemic racism they face each and every day, we have done nothing but fail them at every turn. The trauma they have endured that spans generations is something we must address in a meaningful way, beginning with a full amnesty program for all Aboriginals combined with an apology that must include compensation. Talk alone won't solve their problems.

But one of the most important things she would do is decriminalize drugs. All drugs. Not just weed. It makes so much sense and it's why she's been an outspoken advocate for decriminalization dating back to when she was still in high school. There's simply no rational justification for this radical policy of prohibition. It doesn't stop violence or keep drugs off the streets. Worse yet, it fuels an illicit trade that endangers everyone, leading to mass incarceration that unfairly targets Aboriginals and other marginalized groups. Paisley can only dream of all the good that could be done with the money spent on the so-called war on drugs. Yet even though legalization and regulation is clearly the only way to go, no one at the provincial or the federal level wants to touch it with a 10-foot pole. *What are they scared of? Helping people? Reducing crime?*

The highlight of tonight's meeting was a fascinating presentation on ways to silence the climate-change deniers. Sharifa was such a wonderful speaker and came back with some great ideas from the latest climate summit in Paris where she rubbed shoulders with some of the bigwigs in the United Nations. She handled herself so well even in the face of a rude interruption by some bozo who asked what business she has lecturing us on lowering our carbon footprint while she and other climate champions burn up fossil fuels jet-setting around the world. She just continued on while security had that asshole escorted out. Paisley would have loved to have seen them work him over, though she was at least able to hear the guy moaning and groaning like a little baby in the alley. Serves him right. When he looks in the mirror and sees that black eye and feels those broken ribs, he'll know to keep his big mouth shut. If Paisley had her way, that's the way they'd deal with all the climate-change deniers. But the most talked-about option was modernizing hate-speech laws to allow for the vigorous prosecution of anyone who tries to refute the widely held view of scientists around the globe that man-made climate change is the greatest threat to the planet since the Ice Age. It certainly fits hand in glove with the principle she and her party comrades have long since advocated that only by stopping free speech and freedom of expression can we enforce a more tolerant society. Of course, Paisley would like to take it one step further. Such deplorables should be denied public services like health care, transit and even libraries. There can be no sympathy for any of them.

As the last of the other attendees and committee members make their way out, Paisley packs up her materials and calls for a limo, only to be put on hold. She fumes as she is forced to listen to annoying Muzak. It has been a long night and she is anxious to get home. She thought about bringing her pink Infiniti, but she's always reluctant to take it out in the winter. Even just for a few blocks. It gets so dirty and she hates driving a dirty car. Which is why she uses her ward allowance for limo rides at this time of year. There's no way she'd settle for a cab anymore. One of them that came to pick her up reeked of stale beer and there was dried puke all over the seat. It was awful. Let those taxpayer watchdog groups with nothing better to do who always hound her about spending money get into the back of one of those smelly cabs. And shove that stupid Teddy Waste Award up their ass. Or whatever they call that thing they gave her last year. Needless to say, she didn't take the time to study it closely before chucking it into the garbage. What she really should have done was mail it back to them along with a letter from her lawyer threatening a defamation of character lawsuit. She's getting sick and tired of these vicious personal attacks. Maybe that would shut them up.

Finally someone comes on the line. They tell her they're super busy and she'll have to wait 20 minutes. *Twenty minutes?!* That's totally unacceptable. The hell with that first come, first served policy of theirs. Frequent customers like her should get priority. And they know she's a very important city councilor here on official business. That alone should get her put at the top of the queue. She's going to have to make some phone calls to their head office first thing tomorrow morning. And if she doesn't get the right answers, she'll switch to another service. She's put up with enough shit from them. She's still sore about the time she booked a limo back in September for a girls' night out. They only had *one* bottle of champagne in the back seat. *One!* For all four of them. Worse yet, it was one of those cheap dollar-a-bottle brands. And it wasn't even all that cold. You'd think after a disaster like that they'd be rolling out the red carpet for her when she calls.

At least she can wait inside until the bloody limo comes. And it better be one of those long, white stretch limos. Even if it is just for a three-block ride. She's a good customer, damn it, and expects to be treated accordingly. Along with a bucket of the finest champagne on ice. Surely getting enough ice in this weather shouldn't be a problem. In the meantime, she can visit the washroom. Such as it is. The last few times she's held events at the Earl Grey, the washroom has been absolutely filthy. Time and again, she's complained to the general manager. He says they clean it every day. Sometimes two or three times if there are multiple events in the same day. But that's just bullshit. She's said so right to his face. And she sure didn't like his tone. As a city employee, he ought to know better than to talk down to any councilor, let alone someone of her stature. Luckily, it looks half-decent as Paisley walks in and looks around. The smell isn't even all that bad. Maybe they did finally listen to her after all.

After getting out of the stall, she goes up to the sink and looks at herself in the mirror. *Oh God!* Her hair is all messed up. She can't bear the thought of being seen like that. Even if it's just for the limo driver. So after splashing a little water on her hands and grabbing a paper towel to dry them, she hurriedly pulls out a comb from her purse and gets to work. Finally satisfied, she takes a step back for a good look. *There, that's better.* All it needs now is a few more squirts of hair spray. It'll do until she gets home. But while she's at it, she should check the back. She's certainly got enough time on her hands. Because they're too busy fussing over the lowlifes and creeps to tend to a VIP customer. After pulling out a mirror from her purse, she shrieks once she notices how matted her hair is. It looks like she just rolled out of bed, for Christ's sake. So she grabs the comb once again and starts to tackle that rat's nest her hair has become. *It's just awful!* And as she begins to tackle the tangles, she realizes it's going to take a while. The limo driver will just have to wait. They've made her wait long enough. They can wait for her for once.

Preoccupied with her hair and going over some words in her head for when she reams out the owner of the limo company, she pays little attention to the shadowy figure who has slipped in and has gently closed the latch on the door behind him. She thought the place was empty, but she figures it must be one of the stragglers. "Don't mind me," she says as the man wearing a black balaclava with small holes only big enough for his eyes and his mouth tiptoes ever closer. She is completely caught off guard when the man suddenly wraps his arm around her neck in a choke hold. She tries to scream, but with the man tightening his grip, she can emit nothing more than a tiny squeak. She also cannot breathe. Desperately flailing away at the forearm that is cutting off the oxygen supply to her brain, she feels as helpless as a small child trying to fight off the Incredible Hulk as she falls limply to the floor and loses consciousness. Out like a light, she cannot feel him pressing her index finger on the plunger of a syringe to inject her with a lethal mixture of heroin laced with fentanyl that will kill her before the limo arrives. Nor can she feel him grabbing her by the armpits and dragging her lifeless body back inside the same stall she was just in, where she will spend her final seconds on Earth.

Before the River Heights–Fort Garry council seat becomes vacant.

Chapter 19

Ben

Sunday, January 28, 12:34 AM

It has been a busy couple of days for Ben Podolsky. And now he wants to go home where he can catch up on some much-needed sleep. It all started on Friday afternoon when he met some big shots at the airport who had flown in from out of town for the annual SalesOne conference this weekend. Where many of his company's loyal but obnoxious customers come in to hear about the latest developments in the mission-critical sales-lead tracking software they pay him good money for. And where he, in turn, can get their feedback on what they want from the product. Never in his wildest dreams did he think that the little learning project he developed in his basement would blossom into something so many would find useful, let alone pay him for. Now that antisocial dork off in the corner cubicle who everyone mocked and so many wouldn't hire because of the "wrong" answers he gave to those stupid behavioral interview questions owns his own company. One that employs more than a dozen people working out of an office in the Exchange District serving a customer base in the thousands from all over the world. *Screw the ink blots! And all those HR snobs who told him to take a hike.* He took particular pleasure in sending a biting, sarcastic rejectogram to one of them who had the gall to apply for an open position with SalesOne. *Take that, bitch!*

Of course, it hasn't all been a bed of roses. It's been a grind. Long hours. Hard work. And Winnipeg isn't exactly friendly to the business community. Even he, as a lifelong resident of the city, was surprised by the ridiculous amount of red tape he's had to cut through. No one wants to get anything done in this town. It's no wonder so many people can't wait to get out. The city truly survives only in spite of itself. The taxes sure don't help either. It's a wonder he doesn't get taxed when he goes for a shit. The worst one is the payroll tax. Brought to you by an NDP government that had just started a jobs fund. Then when you hire someone, they slap you with a punitive tax. Only a pea-brained socialist could think that makes sense. Having to schmooze with clients hasn't been easy either. At least for him anyway. But it's part of the job and he's learned to deal with it a little better now, though he still hates it and always will. At his core, he's a geek. He just wants to sit in his cubicle and crank out code. Leave all the business stuff to someone else. But as much as he'd like to do just that, he can't bring himself to do it. He's seen too many cases of dishonest bookkeepers. Years ago, one of his old colleagues had bilked his employer out of over $100,000. And there was that high-profile case of the accounting clerk in Selkirk who ripped off the physiotherapist she worked for. The doc went crazy when he found out and shot her and her husband before turning the gun on himself. That's not going to happen on Ben's watch. And in any event, he's too much of a control freak. He could never bring himself to give anyone else that kind of authority in his company.

The worst part, however, has been all the notoriety. There are times he wishes he could turn back the clock and go back to just being Joe Blow again. He's always been the type of person who wants to come and go and have no one know he was ever there. But the genie is already out of the bottle. There's no going back now. Some of the attention has been positive, he has to admit. It was nice to get that small-business entrepreneur of the year award from the chamber of commerce. Not that he had a whole lot of competition, mind you, since there's so little private-sector development in the city. Just this weekend, when someone from Vancouver asked him what the big industry in Winnipeg was, Ben answered, "Government. Followed closely behind by auto theft." In fact, now that he thinks of it, most of the attention has been positive. There's only been a couple of exceptions. But they've been big ones. He still doesn't like talking about them. Even though he's been offered free counseling from Victim Services, he's only been a couple of times. All it did was dredge up bad memories he'd just as soon forget. In the first case, all he wanted was for the guy to go away. He'd have been happy to drop the charges. But the guy just wouldn't stop. He was a real psychopath. The judge said it was one of the most outrageous cases he'd ever seen. And yet even after all the guy had put Ben through, he still kept going on and on about how *he* was the victim. How Ben was so selfish for not helping him. Just because you put a product out there doesn't give anyone the right to harass the developer at home and threaten him if he doesn't cooperate. It was really scary. And it still is, even after all this time. They would have locked the guy up and thrown away the key if Ben had his way. *Bloody soft judges!* He still has trouble sleeping at night. And everywhere he goes, he's always on high alert wondering if the guy is lurking around somewhere. A restraining order isn't going to help much with a knife to your throat or a gun to your head. Then just when he thought he was out of the woods, lightning would strike twice with another one just like the other guy. The circumstances were different, all right, but it still didn't make it any less hard on Ben. Which sadly, meant another forced move. He wonders if there's something he's doing that attracts people like that.

It was why he refused the free drink the woman at the bar kept offering him. It was probably legitimate. Happens all the time when he's out on these schmooze-fests. But she seemed unusually persistent about it, which made the hair on the back of his neck stand on end. Usually when he says no, that's the end of it. Move on and find another sucker. He's never had to ask the bouncer to step in before. The guys were heckling him about it nonstop for the rest of the night. And maybe he was just being ultra-paranoid. Wouldn't be the first time. But given his past history, it's better to be safe than sorry. Other than all the ribbing, though, it wasn't a bad evening. If one must go out on the town after the conference. Which seems to be part of some unwritten law. Ben avoids restaurants whenever and wherever possible, but the meal at the Old Spaghetti Factory wasn't too bad. He hadn't been there since they moved to the Johnston Terminal at The Forks. The historic junction of the Red and Assiniboine Rivers where the city was founded. Transformed by the government into a tacky destination site with repurposed warehouses, where what few tourists the city manages to attract seem only too happy to pay local artisans an arm and a leg for worthless trinkets they'll never use. Then fork over what little cash they have left for an unforgettable gastronomic misadventure at any of the ethnic restaurants. Ben nearly threw up just looking at that tub of sickly pale-green goop some big burly dude with a long straggly beard and tattoos up and down his arm was stirring with an oar. He wonders how much he would have to be paid to eat that stuff.

Aside from the usual griping about the cold–standard issue for any out-of-town visitor in January–much of the talk at the table centered around the big news story of the day in Winnipeg. A city councilor, Paisley Frankel, was found dead last night at a community center, and although the official cause of death won't be released until after the autopsy, all the reports suggest it was a heroin overdose. Hardly a surprise. She was a well-known druggie and was always front and center whenever the junkies organized a campaign to legalize drugs. Not just weed, but the hard-core stuff like cocaine, LSD and, of course, heroin. Which made it such a fitting way for her to go. Ben almost had to laugh when he heard the news. It was like when the Marlboro Man died of lung cancer. And not to speak ill of the dead, but her death was sure no great loss to the world. She was the typical champagne socialist who always claimed to be looking out for low-income people yet drove around in a luxury car and racked up more limo expenses than any councilor in the city's history. In fact, according to one report, it was a limo driver who found her in the washroom with a needle in her arm and called 911. It couldn't help but remind him of that MLA who was out jogging late at night near the railway tracks and got mugged by a couple of scumbags who were only out of jail thanks to the hug-a-thug policies he championed. From what Ben heard, the guy was beaten to a pulp.

A couple of the guys were still talking about it even after the group left the restaurant and went for a nightcap at the bar in the food hall in the Forks Market. As if any of them needed the extra libation. *God, they like to drink!* Some of them are just as bad as hockey players.

It took more than an hour and a half before the guys finally began trickling out. He appreciates their business and all, but enough is enough already. They can get drunk and booze it up at home. So he was hardly faking the wide grin on his face while glad-handing them as they left in a succession of cabs, headed back to their respective hotels to crash and sober up before flying home in the morning. No doubt taking their hangovers with them. Ben, meanwhile, ventures out onto the frozen tundra separating the Forks Market from the parkade. Where they recently started charging, setting off a furor among cheap Winnipeggers. Cost-sensitive, to be more politically correct. A trait that seems to define those who inhabit the city. So much so that Winnipeg is often used as a test market for new products. If it sells in Winnipeg, it will sell anywhere. And Ben certainly counts himself among the cheap. After years of getting free parking at The Forks, now having to pay really frosts his balls, figuratively and literally. *They could at least build a heated walkway with all the dough they're raking in now. It's not like this is the first time it's gone below freezing in Winnipeg.* He makes a mental note to make sure to save his receipt. He can at least write it off as a business expense.

But before stepping outside into the cold, he first carefully scans from side to side to make sure that woman at the bar isn't around. Thankfully, no one appears to be lurking in the shadows. That's one good thing about this weather. It keeps the crazies inside. On his way across the dimly lit icy concrete pad, Ben's mind also drifts to thoughts of his Dodge. *Will it start after being outside so long in the cold? Have the tires been slashed? Windows broken, maybe? Will it even be there?* Natural questions for any Winnipegger who has left his vehicle unattended for more than five minutes. He knows he doesn't have long before being able to answer those questions as he soon reaches the parkade entrance. To get up to the second level where he left his beater, he must take the elevator or the stairs. With the elevator, he risks being trapped in for the rest of the weekend if the power goes out. But with the stairs, there could be a scumbag or a strung-out junkie in there ready to jump him. Tough choices. *Tell me again why, in the middle of the violent crime capital of North America, they don't have security available to walk you to your car.* And he's got to pick one since scaling the side of the building isn't an option. He's not Spider-Man. After a little thought, applying the theory of the cold keeping the crazies away, he opts for the stairwell.

His gamble pays off as he reaches the second level without incident. Better yet, he can see his Dodge at the opposite end of the deserted lot. Just where he left it. Whether it will start remains an unanswered question, but at least it's still there and, more importantly, looks to be in one piece. That much he can make out in the dark shadows.

His spirits pick up even more when he gets close enough to his Dodge to see that no windows appear to have been broken. And his tires look fully inflated. Studying it closer from a distance, there's no other obvious signs of vandalism. There are no graffiti or gang symbols spray-painted on it. But as he remains preoccupied with his car while fishing the keys out of his pocket, he has failed to notice the masked hooligan with a machete in his hand lurking behind the only other car in the lot, parked a few spots away.

A hooligan waiting just for him.

Chapter 20

Fugitive

Monday, January 29, 7:49 PM

Sierra feels like a fugitive hiding out in the back of a dark, grungy coffee shop. This is the last place on Earth she wants to be right now. But she has no choice. She is desperate. Desperate enough to seek refuge in a place like this that's filthy as hell. There's rat poo under her table. At least she thinks it's rat poo. She's not enough of an expert on poo to tell for sure. Maybe it's mouse poo. But it is definitely poo. And it's disgusting. Right next to it is a bunch of leftovers from someone's meal that the vermin have been feasting on. It makes her feel crawly all over. It's not a whole lot better on top of the wooden table either. It's encrusted with grime. So much so that the cup is actually sticking to the table. If only she didn't actually have to buy something for the privilege of being there. They should have to pay her instead. But right now, it serves her purpose. No one she knows would be caught dead here. And it's convenient. Right around the corner from the short-term rental unit where she's staying. It's more like a dorm, really. She thought it would be great to stay near her alma mater. But it's horrible. Just horrible. It's not very clean and it's so noisy. Students coming and going all the time. The noise isn't something that bothered her when she was one of them. But now, she just wants to go to sleep and forget all this ever happened. Sadly, it was all she could get. More importantly, it's all she can afford right now. She's completely tapped out financially. She's still stuck making the payments on her condo. The one she can't get into or put on the market. Not just her half of the mortgage payment, but the entire amount. And her lawyer, Cammi, needed a retainer. Another reason she needs this whole business to go away and fast.

Of course, anything's better than a jail cell. Which is where she might have been right now if the judge hadn't taken pity on her. She broke down and bawled like a baby in the courtroom this morning when the charges were being read. Cammi thought it might have helped. After Sierra calmed down, she confessed that she was surprised bail was granted at all given the seriousness of the charges and the weight of the evidence against her. But she also thought being a lez and a cop didn't hurt either.

Still nervously awaiting her contact, she casts a glance out toward the street where the snow is gently falling. She watches the people walking by, slipping and sliding on the ice. Sierra almost slid and fell herself when she walked in. But even though they're outside freezing and she's at least inside and warm, she'd still do anything to trade places with any of them. And go back to her normal life. Just like they can. It still blows her mind how her life has been turned upside down in the space of a week.

On the big screen on the wall to her left is some kind of hockey game. At least she thinks it's hockey, for all she knows or cares about it. All she knows is that it involves a bunch of big guys on skates who shoot a ball around and fight a lot. But whatever it is on the screen, everyone in the place is glued to it. Which means they're not focused on her. Someone who has seemingly become the most recognizable figure in the whole city right now. Her picture has been all over the news today and will probably be on the front cover of the papers tomorrow. The cop who drove an ice pick into the skull of a beloved Winnipeg media personality after a lesbian lovers' quarrel got out of hand.

Finally, the door opens and a tall, thin figure comes in from the cold. Much to her relief, it's Ken. Sierra wasn't sure he was even going to come. She was a little surprised Ken even took her call. After all, the two of them aren't exactly the best of friends. And he's among many who think she has no business with a badge. But she didn't know where else to turn. She needs help.

He gives her a nod after spotting her huddled in the back of the room with a scarf around her head like a Muslim woman before stopping at the counter. *He's probably ordering a coffee.* As he grabs the mug, it reminds her she should have warned him to bring his own. He might soon be drinking cockroach poop. But she has a few more pressing things on her mind right now. He approaches the table, pulls out the chair with his free hand and takes a seat.

"Thank you for coming," says Sierra.

Ken responds with a grunt before taking a loud slurp of his coffee. Then he hands her a scrap of paper. There's a phone number on it. "Probably best you don't call my work number again," he mumbles. Sierra doesn't ask, but she figures it's for a burner phone. *Probably the same number he gives informants.*

"You know I shouldn't be here. I could really get hauled on the carpet for even being seen with you, let alone talking to you like this," he says. Before Sierra can respond, he continues, "You're persona non grata around the office, you know. People are scared to even mention your name."

Sierra's jaw drops. Sure, homophobia and sexism remain rampant on the force. She knows that better than anyone. But even those old-school types whose hate knows no bounds ought to know those allegations are completely baseless. She knows that Andrea, of all people, would have no tolerance for that crap. She would be the one person above all others who would support Sierra. More so than even the chief. For sure, if Andrea was in charge of the investigation, there's no way it would have come to this. It's only because that swine Al Hunt saw a golden opportunity to garner some brownie points for the IIU in the media. The hell with who he has to step on to do it. The only reason she didn't call Andrea was that she didn't want to burden her. The poor woman must have a thousand things on her plate. So that's why she called Ken instead. Not to mention that Ken would likely have more of the details Sierra needs. She needs to clear her name. How, she still doesn't know. But the one thing she does know is that she sure can't count on the likes of Al and his team of savages to be objective. She wouldn't put it past them to just make up a bunch of shit. It would be easy enough to do. They've got her fingerprints on file. DNA. Everything.

But that's for another day. She needs to get down to business. Right after she inquires about her boss. Andrea was so helpful that night. Sierra doesn't know how she would have made it through it all without her.

"Andrea," she says. "How's she doing? This must be taking quite the toll on her."

"Sorry to break it to you, but this is all on her direct orders."

Sierra stares at Ken in disbelief. *How dare he say such a thing! Andrea is my friend!* She becomes angry. At Ken. But more at herself. She should have known better than to call him. She can't believe how naive she was. So gullible. Lesson learned, that's for sure. She sure won't make that mistake again. For sure now, she'll have to call Andrea. Andrea is probably worried sick about her. And no doubt, Andrea will fill her in on all she knows about the case. She doesn't need Ken. Ken can go straight to hell. But first, she needs to give him a piece of her mind.

"You're lying!" she yells as she stands up, grabs her purse and awkwardly shoves the metal chair toward the table, making a hell of a racket as the legs scratch against the wooden floor. In the process, she knocks over the half-empty cup she was drinking from, spilling the remaining contents all over the table. Her mini-tantrum has drawn the attention of everyone else in the place, who turn away from the big screen and toward Sierra, whose face has turned beet red. But she's so pissed she doesn't give a shit. *Let them stare!*

"Wish I was," says Ken, who nonchalantly takes another sip of his coffee. "Andrea doesn't give a rat's ass about you. She's just livid that someone in her team has brought negative publicity to her unit."

"That's just not true!"

"Don't believe me? Stop by the front desk tomorrow morning. All your things are in a cardboard box waiting for you. She had someone clean out your desk last week."

"She's really freaking out. Never seen her like that before," he continues as Sierra pauses to take it all in. "The chief too. So many killings in a short period of time is making them look bad."

"Don't take it so personally," he adds as Sierra gently pulls the chair back out and slowly takes a seat. "It's all about PR. Even you with your fairy-tale ideals ought to know that. They'll forgive most anything. Drunk driving. Taking bribes. Dealing drugs. Domestic battery. Just as long as they're able to keep it hush-hush. But once it hits the news, look out. The bosses don't like being made to look bad. Including Andrea."

"But I didn't do anything. I didn't kill Victoria. Or the doctor. Or Leah."

"Doesn't matter."

"I just don't believe people can be that heartless."

"Open your eyes. Look around. You're lucky you're not in the klinker right now. And even if you do ultimately beat the rap, a dollar to a donut says you're done with the Service. You'll always be damaged goods in their eyes. If they're not able to make up some reason to shitcan your ass, they'll bust you down to traffic or have you shuffling papers on the graveyard shift. They'll make it so miserable for you that you'll want to quit."

Sierra hangs her head, blankly staring at the table. All she can hear in the noisy place are the drips from the coffee she just spilled hitting the floor as Ken's words slowly begin to sink in. *Good God, what if he's right?*

After a few more moments of silent introspection, Sierra finally raises her head.

"If everyone is so heartless, then why are you here? Why did you even take my call?"

"Because I know you didn't kill your girlfriend. Or wife. Whatever the two of you are. Were. And I think I know who did."

Chapter 21

The Suspect
Monday, January 29, 7:57 PM

"Go on," says Sierra.

"You know that guy you were looking at in the missing woman case?" replies Ken.

"Yeah. Mitch, um, something. Sorry, can't remember right now. So much has been going on."

"Schubert. Mitch Schubert."

"Right. The ex-husband who was stalking her. He had some anger management issues, but he went for counseling. Still not sure about him, but whatever the case, he has an alibi."

"I'll get to that. But hear me out. You know I was working that case of the doctor who got hit in the alley?"

"I remember. Andrea thought you were full of it."

"Still does. Pulled me off the case, in fact. Even went as far to turn it over to the drug unit after I volunteered to work it on my own time. She still thinks the perp is a junkie. That's what happens when you use Affirmative Action to promote stooges like her into leadership positions. But anyway, before I got the hook, I was going through the good doctor's files. And guess which name came up?"

Fuming over the Affirmative Action remark, all Sierra can do is grunt.

"Schubert."

"So?"

"That was my thought. But then I went through his file. Made for some interesting reading. At least what I was able to read. You know how doctors are with their handwriting."

Sierra forces a smile as Ken continues.

"Dr. Cho was his family doctor, but from his appointment records, it looks like Schubert hadn't seen him for a while. And he hadn't been going to him for all that long. He used to go to some other guy who retired and his file got turned over to Cho."

Sierra stifles a yawn. *Get to the point.*

"Where things really got interesting was when I dug deeper into the file.

Schubert's got a brain tumor. Specialist said it's terminal. Gave him three or four months to live."

Sierra's eyes perk up a little. *He said he was under the weather.*

"Of course, there were pages and pages of stuff. As his family doctor, Cho got copied on everything. And I mean *everything*. Once I got through all that, there were Cho's own notes from Schubert's visits, back to when Schubert first started coming to him with symptoms. Cho didn't think it was much at first. Kept writing prescriptions. It was quite a while before he first sent Schubert to a specialist. Then it was in their hands. Cho never saw Schubert again. But there was more. He wrote that Schubert had been repeatedly calling the office, haranguing the receptionist and demanding to speak to Cho, calling him a murderer along with every other name in the book. Even after the office blocked his phone number, Schubert wouldn't stop. He would call from pay phones. Or forge his caller ID. Then he started showing up at the office. They called the cops once, but he took off before they got there."

So much for that anger management counseling.

"I presented all this to Andrea. I wanted to look into this further, especially in light of Schubert's connection to your missing woman. Bring him in for questioning. But she thought it was nothing. The guy must have had a thousand patients or more, she said. If she had a dollar for every patient who had a beef with his doctor, she could retire tomorrow and live like a queen basking on the beaches in the south of France. That's when she told me I was off the case."

Andrea had a point. But still . . .

"I was going to let it go. Pick your battles, you know. Pass it on to the guys in the drug unit and let them run with it. Until I picked up an old newspaper at a coffee shop and read more about the case of that guy whose car overturned. Paper did a feature on him. He was apparently a well-known figure in the community. Did a lot of volunteer work with kids and stuff. They also mentioned he was a big-shot sales manager for Sinedubio Solutions. Big company. Got offices across Canada and North America."

So?

"Recognize the name?"

"I've seen a few of their ads."

"It's where Schubert works."

Oh, yeah. Now I remember. Might be a coincidence. But that's someone else connected to Schubert who's either dead or missing.

"Found out in Dr. Cho's file. So I started doing a little more digging. Talked to Corazon. She's got your case about the missing woman, by the way. Schubert's ex. She's way out of her league. Spinning around like a top. Doesn't know which way is up. But Andrea wants to give her some rope. It's good to have a visible minority working such a high-profile case, she said. That's why she moved Corazon to the head of the table. Right next to her. The new teacher's pet."

Hey, that's my spot!

"Anyway, she was happy to let me look through the file. She didn't ask why, but I said I was looking for another case that might have some relevance. And in there was the stuff you uncovered about the stalking case Schubert was involved in. Remember?"

"Of course."

"Well, guess who testified against him?"

"Sorry."

"Winston Grayson."

Who?

"The hit-and-run case last week. Just off Isabel Street. It hasn't made the papers, but they finally got an ID on the stiff and it's Grayson, all right. A buddy in the traffic division told me and I remembered the name from the file. Family and friends reported him missing. Unfortunately, there's no witnesses. Talked to people in the area, but no one saw anything. Got a couple of paint chips though. They're checking out body shops since the perp's car probably got damaged, but they're not terribly optimistic. Those guys are pretty tight-lipped, and the cops in this town aren't exactly highly regarded if you know what I mean."

Oh God!

Sierra takes a moment to process everything.

"You mentioned the alibi."

"Right. Tommy Anderson. The mentally challenged guy with the peg leg. From your notes. So I was going to pay him a visit last night. Maybe say I was a friend of Schubert or something. But just as I was walking up to the front door of the block, who comes hobbling out but Mr. Peg Leg. I mean, I didn't ask him for ID or anything, but it had to have been him. So I made myself scarce, then followed him into the coffee shop down the street where he met up with a buddy of his. Kid has a loud voice. Didn't exactly need a microphone to be able to hear him."

"And?"

"Well, the guy kept blabbering about how he hadn't seen his friend in a while and hoped he wasn't in trouble or anything. Then after a while, he blurted out that he had covered for him when the cops called. Didn't mention Schubert by name, but let's face it, how many friends does a guy like that have in his social circle? As he rambled on, it sounded like Schubert fed the kid a line about some people making up lies about him and asked him to say he was with him that night."

Wow!

Sierra takes a deep breath.

"OK. There's a kook out there who's settling a bunch of old scores. Including Leah. My case. But still, what's the connection to Victoria? She knew a lot of people obviously, but I never heard her mention Schubert at all. I've been through her contact list and I don't remember ever seeing his name in there."

"I looked into that. And you're right, there's no apparent connection. Well, none that I've found so far. Except for one."

"What's that?"

"You."

Me?

"You interviewed him, didn't you? You talked about it at the meeting and it was in your notes. You put a detail on him."

Yeah.

"Consider this. I know it sounds a little far-fetched. But bear with me. Let's say he spots the detail and gets spooked. He figures you're onto him. He's got to get you off his back. So he kills your girlfriend. That would do it. At least for the time being. Sure sends a hell of a message."

"But why not just kill me? Why Victoria?"

"Good question. Let me ask you, where were you that night?"

"At a hotel. The Four Points."

"The two of you were having problems?"

"Yeah."

"And your girlfriend was home alone?"

"As far as I know. I mean, maybe she had someone else with her. Another girl maybe. Or even a guy for all I know."

"And are you in the phone book?"

"Um, yeah."

"The phone's in your name?"

"Yeah."

"Well, there you have it."

"That's how he found me."

"Exactly. He might very well have been targeting you. How was he supposed to know you were at the hotel?"

A chill goes up Sierra's spine.

"God, I might still be in his crosshairs. He's got to know by now that I'm still alive and that he killed Victoria instead. I mean, it's been all over the news and everything."

"True. But he might have bigger fish to fry now that you're off the force and facing problems of your own. Still, watch your back. You still have your gun?"

"No, I had to turn it in."

"Get another one."

"But it's not legal, now that I'm on leave."

"Murder isn't legal either."

Sierra grudgingly nods in agreement.

"I'll hook you up with a guy. Keep it with you at all times. Schubert is out there. And remember, he's got nothing to lose."

Chapter 22

A Plan

Monday, January 29, 9:12 PM

Still contemplating all that Ken had to say, Sierra stares blankly at the wall at the back of the coffee shop amid all the cheering. Someone must have scored a home run. Or a goal. Whatever it is they do that gets them so worked up. Sierra just doesn't get it. But then again, she's got a lot more on her mind than hockey right now. Like that a homicidal maniac wants her dead. That in addition to the fact that he butchered her fiancée in cold blood and she's the primary suspect.

At first, she was skeptical. *Could it really be true?* Even Ken admitted some of it was a little far-fetched. Maybe his imagination was running wild. It happens all the time. But the more she thought about it, it made sense. All the pieces fit. Everyone who has ever crossed swords with this guy is turning up dead. And she might very well have been among them if she had been at home instead of at the hotel that night.

She asked Ken if he knew anything about the security camera. Surely having his face on camera entering the block would force IIU's hand. Make them go after the real killer instead of her. But he heard from one of his contacts that they checked the camera, but the SD card had been stolen. Easy enough to do, he said. Just pop it out. Cheapest thing on the market. Something she knows all too well. Last year, the HOA proposed a more elaborate system with all the bells and whistles including online storage. But the homeowners voted it down. Too much money, they said. This is a good neighborhood. What do we need all this for? No wonder they keep calling Winnipeg a discount town.

Still, she thought they had enough to take to Andrea. Surely she would listen this time and go to bat for her with IIU. Even if there was only a remote chance all of this was true. Ken said he tried. But she just wouldn't listen. She said she was pleased with the progress Corazon is making on the Leah case and didn't want to interfere. Corazon needs this experience, she said. As for all the other stuff, she said it was all fantasy. The drug unit's working the Dr. Cho case now, and there's no evidence of foul play in either traffic case. Accidents happen all the time on icy highways and there's seemingly a hit and run every week in the city. Just a matter of time before the driver comes forward and cops to it, she said. She seemed somewhat intrigued by the common connection though. But Winnipeg is a small town, she said. If you look hard enough, you can find a link between just about any two people in the city. Then she told him he was thinking too much and to go home and get a good night's sleep. Even Sierra had to roll her eyes when she heard that. She couldn't believe Andrea could be so callous. It made her want to cry. And when the tears started flowing, she just couldn't stop them. It was like Niagara Falls. Probably everyone in the bar could hear her bawling like a baby. She was so embarrassed. She just wanted to put a bag over her face and run out of there.

Even Ken felt sorry for her. He even came over to put his hands on her shoulders. Gave her a napkin off the table to dry her eyes. But after calming down, she still has to face the reality that she's on her own without a clue as to what do to. She doesn't even know where to start. Ken suggested hiring a better lawyer for starters. That in addition to going to see Ken's gun guy later tonight. *Why do they always want to meet in an alley in the middle of the night?* Keep it locked and loaded and with you at all times, he said. Don't even go to the bathroom without it. No telling what Schubert will do or where he'll turn up.

Ken had another idea. Start following Schubert around. Stake him out. Might just get lucky. Because he's bound to strike again. He's not done. Not by a long shot. He'll keep killing until the cancer eats him to the bone. Maybe Sierra won't be the target. But someone else sure will be. And Ken thought he knew who might be next on his list. Ben Podolsky. Sierra instantly recognized the name. His name was all over the file because he was the guy Schubert was stalking. Next logical target, Ken said. If Schubert did the guy who testified against him in court, for sure he'll go after Podolsky too. Save the best for last. That is, if Schubert hasn't done him already. Ken said he'd been trying to reach Podolsky all day. No answer at home, and the receptionist at his office said she doesn't know where he is. But if Podolsky is indeed still alive, that might be her ticket to catching Schubert in the act. And maybe, while she's at it, she'll be able to save Podolsky's life in addition to her own.

All this intrigue is making her head spin. She'd much rather leave this to someone else. But she has no choice. She's got to find Mitch Schubert.

Before he finds her.

Chapter 23

Petra and Patrick

Tuesday, January 30, 9:51 AM

Even though she's only been in the waiting room for a few minutes, Petra Mitrovic is already bored. It feels like she's been there for, like, over an hour. She has the patience of nothing. It's all part of her ADHD. The reason she's there in the first place. It all started more than a year and a half ago. When she had the anxiety attack over having to fill out too much paperwork and had to go on sick leave. At first, she was planning on only a four-week absence. Much like she did last time, when she was able to spend the time in British Columbia visiting friends, sightseeing and spending some much-needed time in the spa. But her manager is an idiot. Just like everyone else there. And the entire public service, for that matter. When it came time to extend her sick leave, rather than give her some administrative help to accommodate her disability, he said he needed her to fill out more paperwork. But it was the paperwork that was making her sick. It was no wonder her blood pressure was a little high when she went to see her doctor, who said she couldn't go back to work until they came up with an accommodation plan. So when the sick leave ran out, she was forced to file a grievance. After all, it's a clear case of discrimination. That's what set off the endless round of hearings. They offered mediation, but she wasn't interested. It put her through so much stress. It was why she was so relieved when the disability insurance payment came. That way, she was able to go to Arizona in addition to Mexico. She went by herself. No husband, no boy and no dog. And she missed the dog most. If only she could get rid of her husband and the boy, she'd be fine. The last hearing was a 45-minute session with her manager. She prepared a big PowerPoint presentation to highlight the key points of her case, yet they still want to take it to a master trial. Which is, like, why she's there today to meet with the union lawyer. He seems to be good. But she wishes she could use her brother instead. He's a well-known attorney who has represented unions. All the union bosses think the world of him. He'd be excellent working a case like this. No one knows how to cook the books like him, they say. But even without him, just the Mitrovic name itself can't help but work in her favor. There's nothing that gets employers in this town shitting their pants like having to face off against a Mitrovic. Makes her feel even better about keeping her maiden name.

All this could have been avoided, however, if only she had been able to collect a disability pension. She's certainly more than entitled for having to deal with all that paperwork. Every penny of it. Her only worry there would be how much money she could make while on it. Because she's still got her eye on that provincial director's job. She sent in her 31-page CV last month, but she hasn't heard from them yet. If she doesn't get a call in the next week or so, she'll call up the deputy minister. No reason for them to sit on it for this long. Particularly since there's no candidate out there who's more knowledgeable in her field than she is. Sure, she asked for a lot more than the top end of the range they posted. But she knows they can rustle up more cash. Especially for her. There's no shortage of money in government. You just have to look for it. She even suggested some options for them in her cover letter. In the meantime, she's been supplementing her income by working in the family business. Bloomers Garden Center. Even in winter time, there's plenty to do in the greenhouse. Paid under the table, of course. She wouldn't want to be caught double-dipping.

If only all that manual labor would help keep that weight off. She lost 30 pounds to get down to 220, but since then, she's put it all back and then some. She looks as big as a house now. Like when she was pregnant with Lucas. It's got to be all the stress she's been under. She just can't keep herself from chugging down those tubs of ice cream. Chocolate mocha is, like, her favorite. She went through two of them that day she binge-watched eight *Fast and Furious* movies. Even though she knows all that ice cream is bad for you. The doctor told her as much the last time she was in the emergency room. That was the night she thought she was having a heart attack. It was awful. But after the ambulance rushed her to the hospital, they ran a bunch of tests and said she was OK. Doctor said to just, like, take it easy. And to keep taking her meds. All of them. They're what keep her going. Good thing she still has her cleaning lady coming in twice a week. There's no way she'd be able to keep house all on her own, even after going on sick leave.

Since that time, she's really gotten into photography. But she needs to find more hobbies. Especially now that the boy is, like, back in school. She started with management courses. She tried kickboxing. Took the boy to one of them too. There was a role at her camera club she thought about volunteering for. But she's so unreliable. And she can't stand the club president. The dude is, like, slow. Not slow as in retarded. But just slow. She just can't deal with people who aren't as wired up as she is. She also thought about redoing her kitchen. That would sure keep her occupied for a while. And it needs work anyway. Everything's so dated. The granite countertops look awful. She would much rather have quartz. She got a designer in for a couple of hours to give her some ideas. She needed a fresh pair of eyes because she can think herself stupid. But just like everything else, she never followed through. All part of her ADHD, her therapist tells her. Start a bunch of things but never finish any of them.

Right now, she should be going over her notes and gathering her thoughts before meeting with the lawyer instead of mindlessly staring out the window looking down at the traffic at Portage and Main. But she still can't get Patrick out of her mind. Her Patrick. *How could things have gone so wrong?* She did so much for him. She was nice to him. She bought him gifts. At Valentine's Day. And at Christmas. He's a sucker for Snoopy, so she gave him a big box of Snoopy comic books. All, like, wrapped up with a pretty little bow-tie on it. Yet he didn't even seem grateful when she came by his office to deliver it after her husband left for work. This after doing all that work in his garden one day last summer. She noticed he could use some mulch and color, so when she had the truck, she came by and planted and spread it for him. She would have done the back yard too if only he had left the gate unlocked. OK, he did say he didn't want her to come. But she knows Patrick. He just didn't want her to fuss. That's all he meant. So she went ahead and surprised him anyway. That was such a lovely flower bed she did in his front yard. She spent so much time on it. She wanted it to be perfect for him. And instead, he just went in there with a bloody shovel and tore it up. Even left all the bits of the flowers right there instead of putting them in the bin. As if to show her. *That's gratitude for you!*

Then there was all the stuff with his parents. She asked him over and over again when she could meet them. But each time, he would just blow her off. Heck, he wouldn't even invite her to his house. And she has absolutely no idea why. She had sent his father a card the first time he was in the hospital. The next time he was laid up, she sent a few books along for him to read. She even threw in a box of chocolates. The good stuff too. Not just the regular crap they sell at the dollar store. At least he'd have some nice treats while he was in there. That hospital food is so bad it can kill you faster than the reason you got taken there in the first place. Petra also tried calling Patrick's mother. Wanted to ask if all was well with her husband. And to see if she was all right. She had a scare of her own. Had to go to the emergency room. Something to do with her heart. That's all Patrick would say. Yet Petra could never get through. Each time, there was an automated message saying the number was unavailable. Maybe the line was down. So even though she preferred a formal introduction through Patrick, she decided to drive out there and introduce herself after finding their address in the phone book. Patrick sure wouldn't tell her where they lived. Every time she asked, he danced around it like it was some tightly guarded state secret. Once she got to the front door, she rang the bell. Then she knocked on the door. Several times. But there was no answer. Their car was in the driveway. They had to have been home. Maybe they just didn't hear her, she thought. Old people sometimes are hard of hearing. Before her father died, she practically had to scream at him to be heard. So she went back the next day. Same deal. This time, she went next door to ask one of the neighbors. The neighbor thought they were home and didn't know why they weren't answering. So before going all that way again, Petra asked Patrick about it. Surely he'd know something. But as soon as she mentioned going out there, his face turned white as a sheet. He almost started shaking. She had to ask if he was all right. Then the next day, she got an email from him asking her not to contact his parents again. *What the hell was the problem?* It's a free country. She can go see whoever she wants. She sure as hell doesn't need his permission. It was so strange. Like he was creeped out or something.

Honestly, she just can't figure that guy out. And if that wasn't weird enough, there was that time at the camera club's craft sale when she had a table selling her pictures. She saw Patrick walk in. Watched as he went around from table to table. And yet the bastard didn't come to see her. Didn't even look in her direction. Petra was so mad. She couldn't believe he could be so rude. If she had someone else to man her table, she would have run out into the parking lot and smacked him before he had a chance to take off. *How dare he blow me off!* She had calmed down by the time she saw him again a couple of weeks later. But she was still hot. The worst part was that he didn't even apologize when she confronted him about it. He almost seemed proud of it, in fact. So she told him right then and there she would punch him in the face if he didn't stop and see her at the next craft sale. She didn't give a shit who heard her.

This whole business with Patrick is driving her completely bananas. *What have I done? Why won't he come back to me?*

She has missed Patrick. She needs to get back in his good graces. And get things back to normal. The way they used to be.

One way or another.

Chapter 24

One Left

Tuesday, January 30, 6:33 PM

Over the last couple of weeks, Mitch has sure made himself the talk of the town.

First, there was Leah. His handiwork made the front page. And it's still in the news. Followed by the doctor. That one sure got tongues wagging too. But nothing like when he did Vickie C. He still feels bad about doing her. But in his wildest dreams, there's no way he could have envisioned how well things have turned out. Mitch can't help but laugh. The cops just don't have a clue. Brent and Winston, on the other hand, barely registered on the radar. As he expected. People wipe out all the time on icy highways. All that surprised him was how many people felt sorry for that asshole. Reading all those flowery tributes made him sick to his stomach. They should have thrown a party instead. Guy was pure pond scum who's going straight to hell. And a pedestrian getting nailed in a hit and run is hardly newsworthy. Happens every day in this town, so it seems. Big fat hairy deal.

But Mitch was right back in the headlines once again after they found Paisley Frankel's body. That'll teach her for blowing him off. All the times he's complained to her office. All she'd say is thank you for your patience. Don't get your shit in a knot, in other words. It got to the point that she wouldn't even bother to respond. *Wonder how fast things would get taken care of if you lost a wheel in a pothole. Or couldn't get out of your driveway because your street hasn't been plowed in a couple of months. Get out of your goddamned limo for a change!* Mitch couldn't have been happier to have the honor of administering the last rites. A nice little shot in the arm of a lethal concoction he prepared. Just for her. And as he expected, they're just chalking it up as an overdose. After all, she was perhaps Winnipeg's most famous druggie. They're not even bothering to investigate. Not that there's any reason to. Removing her from the gene pool should hardly be considered a crime. One less fat-cat councilor gorging herself at the public trough. If only he had more time, he'd like to take them all out.

They were so busy fawning over the dearly departed councilor that no one noticed Mitch's latest handiwork. And to be fair, someone getting knifed in the Cityplace parking garage after dark qualifies as another big yawn in this town. There's a stabbing almost every day, and most of them take place within a two-mile radius of Cityplace. But he was a little surprised his effort a little later that night didn't draw more attention. Then again, it was in the back alley of a pretty lousy neighborhood. Drug deals and stuff go on there all the time. Mitch himself picked up a couple of dime bags not too far from there before. Which was why he knew the area and where best to ambush the asshole. Bugger never saw it coming. Knocked him out cold, then stuffed him in his car and drove it into the garage, closed the door and let the carbon monoxide fumes finish him off. Couldn't have gone any smoother. The best part is that the cops are just rubber-stamping it as a suicide. They're not even *suspecting* foul play. Taking the easy way out like the lazy government bureaucrats they are.

Mitch only wishes he could have made the guy suffer more. He didn't deserve to die peacefully in his own garage. Mitch would have loved to have watched him writhe in pain as he drove a knife into his belly and twisted it around, slicing through his innards and slowly draining the life out of him. It would have been fitting punishment indeed for all the grief he caused Mitch ever since the accident. Lying to the police. And to MPI. Going as far as doctoring the footage from his dashcam that would have proven Mitch's innocence. That was unforgivable. He was the one who ran the red light, not Mitch. And the worst part about it was that the adjuster bought the guy's story. Jennifer something. Mitch can't even remember her full name. A real snotty bitch. Didn't even chalk it up as 50/50 like they usually do. So it was Mitch's insurance rates that went up instead of his. Along with getting a few demerits on his license. That's why it was even more satisfying when Mitch knifed her in the gut right after she got off work before leaving her on the cold concrete floor of the parkade to drown in her own blood. He'd loved to have hung around longer. Not only to watch her die but to make sure she knew who delivered her to her maker. As far as she knew, it could have been anyone on a laundry list full of people she's pissed off. But it was a risk he couldn't afford to take. Too many people around there. So he just grabbed her purse and got out of there. Made it look like a simple robbery.

And for sure no one will notice Mitch's most recent conquest. It was so dark on his way back home that Mitch himself barely noticed. Some bum was staggering all over the road. Probably an Indian who had a few too many. It wasn't Mitch's intention, but what the hell. The opportunity was there. All it cost him was a dent in the passenger-side door. He won't bother getting it fixed. The Asmundsons can file a claim with MPI when they get back. All they'll have to pay is the deductible. They can afford it.

But as much good as he's done, the one person who most deserves to be removed from the world of the living is still on the loose. He thought he had Podolsky dead to rights in the parking lot. It was just the two of them. One on one. Mano a mano. One time for all time. He had the machete all sharpened up and ready to go. Behead the bastard with one good swing. Send his head rolling across the lot like a bowling ball. *Steeee-rike!* Then slice him to pieces. Spill his blood all over the lot. Even chop up some of the bones if he could. Once he was finished, they'd have to identify the body using DNA. And when he met his maker, he would have no one to blame but himself. All Mitch had wanted was for the guy to answer some questions for him. That's all. Nothing more. Just a little cooperation. Surely that wasn't too much to ask. Maybe they could have even worked together. But noooo, Mr. Big Shot had to call the police. Then he filed a bunch of trumped-up charges. Gets a few customers and all of a sudden he thinks he's too good for the rest of us peons.

If only Mitch hadn't blacked out right when he was ready to pounce. Couldn't have come at a worse possible moment. Strictly speaking, it shouldn't have even come to that. It was only a backup plan to be used in case the whore he paid to deliver the lethal cocktail in the bar didn't get the job done. *Fucking bitch! I knew she'd let me down!* He even bought her a nice outfit for the occasion so she'd look somewhat respectable. Threw in some extra cash so she could get her hair done too. And all he got was a bunch of whiny excuses. What was I supposed to do, force it down his throat, she asked? *Damn it, I paid for results.* So when she wouldn't give his money back, he slit her throat right there in the alley. Then he stuffed her in the dumpster. Right about now, she's probably making a good meal for the buzzards at the Brady Road dump as they peck away at her rotting flesh.

In the meantime, Mitch has another plan. A much more ingenious one. It has to be. Because Podolsky will be on the lookout. And this one will be foolproof. No way he can get out of it this time. He's going down. And he's going down hard. Mitch will see to that. It's too bad he'll have to take out so many others in the process. But it can't be helped. There's no other way. And besides, everyone dies in the end. It's just a matter of how you go out.

Mitch needs to get to work right away. He'd love to do it tonight if he could. But there are logistics to arrange. And he's wiped out. His energy level is declining by the day, and keeping up this schedule would be tough even if he were completely healthy.

But one thing's for sure, the clock is ticking on dear old Ben Podolsky. In just over 24 hours' time, he will be nothing more than a handful of ashes. Barely enough to coat the end of a shovel.

Mitch can't wait to do the honors.

Chapter 25

Stakeout
Wednesday, January 31, 9:11 PM

Shivering like crazy inside her Taurus, Sierra puts down the paper cup half full of a Starbucks latte and again wipes off the steam from inside the windshield so she can see what's going on across the street. Or what isn't going on. Aside from the handful of people coming and going from the comedy club in the shopping center behind her, there's been absolutely nothing. Well, unless a couple of old ladies coming back from bingo night at the nearby community club counts. She's not really surprised either. After all, who the hell wants to go out in this cold? The wind chill is supposed to get down to −35 overnight. And there's another storm on the way. Anywhere between five and 10 centimeters of the white stuff by morning. Should make for a great commute. *Welcome to Manitoba!*

She's been camped out there ever since the sun went down. In exactly the same spot she was last night. And once again, she's bored as hell. No wonder the guys always whine and complain about being assigned to stakeout duty. Nothing to do besides play games on your phone. And log on to porno sites. So many of them get hit with G-20 violations. Inappropriate use of Internet resources. Sure, there are filters in place. But they always find ways around them. She'd much rather be curled up in bed reading a book. But she needs to catch Mitch Schubert red-handed. It's her only chance. And the only way she's going to be able to find him is to stake out Ben Podolsky's condo. Assuming Mitch hasn't already killed the guy. Like Ken, Sierra's tried to find Ben. Called his office. Secretary said he's working from home. So she rang his phone. But it goes right to voice mail. It's like his phone is turned off. But if Ben is alive, Mitch is bound to show up sooner or later. If, in fact, Mitch really is Winnipeg's answer to Ted Bundy. It still seems so unreal. Especially after what Ken had to say earlier today. First, he told her the MPI adjuster who got stabbed the other night had handled a case involving Mitch. And the other party in that case was just found dead in his garage. A suicide. *Or maybe not.* Then, this afternoon after Paisley Frankel's funeral, he told her he'd found a bunch of angry emails from Mitch in Paisley's inbox. She can't even fathom the possibility that Mitch had anything to do with that dear woman's death. Even Jack the Ripper on his worst day couldn't be that heartless. And Ken admitted that Mitch was far from the only one who had been filling her inbox with vitriol. It makes Sierra so angry. All those right-wing extremists know how to do is spread hate. She certainly shares Paisley's views that it's high time for much tougher hate-speech laws in this country. Throw the whole bloody lot of them in jail and throw away the key. Give them nothing but bread and water and make them crush rocks with their bare hands.

So many who eulogized her today said just that. And it's just one of many honorable causes Paisley would have spearheaded once she became premier. She would have made Manitoba the envy of the nation. Sierra still can't believe she's gone. It's such a loss. Not just for Winnipeg and Manitoba, but for all of us. The world needs more people like Paisley Frankel. Shining lights in a sea of darkness. And yet there are those who actually seem happy about her tragic passing. One columnist said Manitoba dodged a bullet and called her a drug addict who would have driven the province right into the gutter. It takes all kinds. Morons like that make Sierra completely lose faith in humanity.

After drying her eyes, Sierra turns her attention back to the block. A block she can't see until wiping off the windshield once again. And a block whose residents are obviously hunkered down for the night. Just like she should be, since no one has come or gone for the last hour or so. *This is for the birds! I give up!* She should have known better. She's no good at these clandestine stakeouts and far-out conspiracy theories. *There's got to be a better way!* Maybe she needs to talk to Ken again. Or someone else. Cammi perhaps. See what she's got to say about all this. More than anything, Sierra needs a sounding board. She feels like she's all alone, drifting on a two-by-four in the middle of the ocean without a paddle.

She puts down the latte and reaches for the ignition. She needs to get the hell out of there. Go somewhere and clear her head. But just as she goes to turn the key, she spots the lights from a truck turning off Tuxedo Boulevard and headed her way. Wiping away the steam from the windshield once again, she sees it's a white cube van. Probably from the gas company, she thinks. A poof truck, as her uncle would say. Because every time one of those trucks show up, he says, there's an explosion. *Poof!* Sierra watches with interest as the truck turns into the parking lot. *Finally some activity! At least it will keep me from falling asleep. But what a hell of a time to lose your heat. Hopefully it's nothing too serious. Whatever the problem is, at least someone's here to fix it.* She watches that someone pull open the driver-side door and step outside. He's bundled up from head to toe in a big, bulky snowmobile suit with his hood up and a black balaclava covering his face. *Can't have enough layers on in this weather.* She doesn't know how people manage having to work outside at this time of year. *Whatever they're getting paid, it can't be enough.* Then he carefully looks around the lot and even down the street. As if he thinks he's under surveillance or something. *Odd.* As he grabs some equipment from inside the truck, Sierra also finds it odd that he doesn't have a partner with him. Usually there's a couple of guys on each job. Maybe even three or four. Maybe they're short-staffed, she thinks. Or they just don't want to pay any more OT than they have to. With a small box in his hand, he goes over to the front of the building. *Probably where the gas meter is.* She digs out her binoculars for a closer look. She finds it strange that he doesn't have any tools with him. He's just planting the box on the wall next to the meter. *Maybe they're installing a new meter? But why at this time of night? This is the kind of thing they'd do during the day.* Still peering out from her binoculars, she watches the workman go back to his truck and drive to the far end of the lot, parking right alongside the electrical transformer. *What would he be doing there?* She knows the gas company and the power company merged, but they don't have electricians working on gas lines and vice versa. It suddenly dawns on her. *He's gotta take a piss.* Which reminds Sierra that she needs to go as well. The latte has gone right through her. She used the washroom in the grocery store a couple of hours ago. She hopes it's still open. Otherwise, she'll have to go over to the comedy club. As much as she doesn't want to go outside again, she knows she must. So she zips up her coat and steps out of her car and into the deep freeze.

After locking the door, she looks back toward the workman in the parking lot. Under the dim lights, she can't tell exactly what he's doing as he goes back and forth to the truck. But it certainly doesn't look like he's there to take a piss. So before heading over to the little girls' room, she scampers across the street to take a closer look. Crouching down to try to stay out of sight as she makes her way alongside the building to the back of the lot, she can see him hauling some stuff out of the truck. *What the hell is he doing?* She begins to realize this is no workman. It could, in fact, be *him*. Whether it is *him* or not, she knows she can't afford to take a chance. So as her heart begins racing, she feels for the gun inside her right coat pocket. The one she got the other day. The one that's a hell of a lot more powerful than her old police-issued model. *No wonder the guys from the SWAT team are always complaining about getting outgunned on the streets.*

At the rear edge of the building, Sierra kneels down behind an SUV, only a stone's throw from the truck. She can see it clearly. And it's not from the gas company. She's seen enough of their trucks around town. Their name and logo aren't even on it. Just some name on the front door that she can't make out. Could be a delivery truck for all she knows. But this guy sure isn't making a delivery. And he's not there visiting someone. Whoever he is, he's up to no good. *But what should I do? Call Ken? Call 911?* Sadly, she knows there's no time for that, if indeed her instinct is correct. She's got to take care of him herself. But what if she's wrong? She's a suspended cop facing a murder charge with an illegal gun in her possession. *That'll look good.* She turns away and leans back against the SUV's rear tire to try to collect her thoughts as her heart pounds like a drumbeat.

Trying to summon up the courage, she takes a deep breath. *I'm a big girl now.* She reaches into her pocket and pulls out the gun. She takes off the safety catch and loads a round into the chamber before putting it back in her pocket. She keeps her right hand on the handle as she peers around the corner. She looks around. She can't find him. *Where the hell'd you go?* She knows he's around. He didn't just disappear into thin air. She has to find him. So she makes a beeline from the SUV to the rear of the truck. After pausing for a second to catch her breath, she peers around to the driver's side, then back over to the passenger's side. *Still no sign of him.* Maybe he's on the other side of the transformer, she thinks. She'll have to go around to the front of the truck. The lights in the parking lot are shining on the driver's side, so she decides to use the passenger's side. It's covered in darkness and there's only a thin passageway between the truck and the fence. That way, she won't be seen or be ambushed. Stepping gingerly, being careful not to trip and fall, but also not to make too much noise as her boots crunch on the ice, she makes her way alongside the truck to the front door. Looking around the corner, she can see the transformer clearly. And a shadow behind it. That's got to be him, she thinks. Her only choice is to approach from the rear. If he decides to run, she'll be able to flush him out into the open where it's lit. At least she'll be able to see him. Drawing her gun, she scurries over to the back of the transformer. Crouched down, she steps over to the far corner, where she firms up her grip on the gun with both hands. As she readies herself to confront him, a gloved hand comes out of the shadows and slams her head against the side of the transformer. Dazed, she falls to the ground and drops the gun.

The last thing she sees before blacking out is the dark silhouette of a size 12 steel-toed Sorel boot headed right for her skull.

Chapter 26

Prisoner

Friday, February 2, 3:34 PM

Sierra wakes up. But she is still very groggy. She feels as if she's in a fog. She has no idea where she is, what time it is or even what day it is. Nor does she know how long she's been out. It feels like years. The last thing she remembers is being in a dark place. Where it was cold. That's all she can piece together. She does know she has been blindfolded and that she is lying on a bed, spread-eagle with both hands and ankles tied to each of the four bedposts, not with handcuffs, but with a cloth wrap. So tightly, in fact, that she has almost no feeling in her fingers or her toes. Her awareness of the pain from the beating she has taken slowly grows. For starters, she has one hell of a splitting headache. Her cheekbones are throbbing. As more of her senses return, she is filled with the nauseating taste of dried blood. She knows she must look awful. She hopes no one can see her, wherever she is. She might die of embarrassment before she dies of the injuries from the beating. *Someone please put a bag over my head!* Moving farther down, her ribs ache. No doubt they're broken, she thinks. There's also a deep throbbing pain in her thighs and in her crotch. *Oh God!* She doesn't even want to think of what might have happened there. At least she was out when it happened. Or maybe she just doesn't remember it. Either way, it was a blessing. Above all else, she is bitterly cold. She feels like she's being kept in a meat locker. Left there to die. Wearing nothing more than what feels like some flimsy negligee. Probably something that came from a sleazy mail-order catalog like one of her old girlfriends dressed up in one night. All white with pink lace. If only she were back with her now. *Calgon, take me away!*

She hears the click of a door handle. The hinges squeak as the door slowly opens. She follows the sound of loud footsteps around to the foot of the bed. *Clump, clump, clump. They aren't dress shoes. Something a little softer. Probably winter boots with rubber soles.*

Then the clumping stops.

"Awake, I see," says a cheerful male voice. "You've been a real sleeping beauty lately."

"Who are you?" she strains to ask. Her throat is parched.

He doesn't answer. But she knows there's something vaguely familiar about that voice. She can't quite place it. Then it comes to her. *Damn, Ken was right after all!*

"Mitch. You're Mitch Schubert."

"Very good, detective. I'm impressed. Took you for a quota hire. Guess I was wrong."

As her brain begins to connect the dots while she listens to Mitch clang a couple of cups around and open a dresser drawer, something else creeps back in her mind.

The likely possibility that this is the man who killed Victoria.

"Victoria," she ekes out in a scratchy voice. "Did you kill Victoria?"

He doesn't answer.

"You did, didn't you?" she asks as her blood pressure begins to skyrocket.

He still doesn't answer.

"Answer me!" she shrieks.

"Couldn't be helped, babe."

Couldn't be helped? And I'm not your "babe"!

"Why? What did she do to you?"

"Mistaken identity. Didn't mean to."

Didn't mean to? You drove an ice pick through her skull a gazillion times!

"There's no way I'd have done her if I had known. She was cool. Had no idea the two of you were shacking up. Didn't even know she was a switch-hitter. But I guess I'm not surprised. She did like playing the field, if you know what I mean."

"But hey, it still worked out so well," he continues. "At least I thought so. You and the cops were out of my hair. I was in the clear. But damn, don't you show up in the strangest places."

Strange place? Oh yeah, behind a building somewhere.

"All I needed was a few more minutes. Everything would have been taken care of. But nooooo. You had to show up. Ruining everything I had so carefully planned. Had to grab you and get the hell out of Dodge before the cavalry showed up."

Cavalry? There was just me.

"Is this where you took Leah?" she asks softly.

"Good guess, detective. You were onto me pretty early there. Got to give you credit on that one. But, of course, you had no evidence."

"Is she here?"

"Well, sort of."

What does he mean, she asks herself as she listens to the clumping of his feet, first going around to the left side of the bed before growing fainter. *Probably gone to get something.* She doesn't have long to wait to find out what he's up to as he returns in a jiffy. She hears him go around to the right side of the bed, then she feels the mattress shake after he throws down something heavy right next to her. Something cold.

He rips down the blindfold. Her bloodshot eyes are instantly drawn to the huge glass jar at her side. *A big pickle jar perhaps?* She can't tell, since her vision is still blurry. It feels like she's been blindfolded for, like, forever. *Whatever it is, it looks all frosted up. Probably came right from the freezer.* All she can make out is that there's something black near the top of the jar. *Could be anything.*

"Care to hazard a guess?" he asks as struggles to twist the top off the jar. Having finally gotten it loose, he tosses the top between Sierra's prone legs and sticks one hand inside to try to pry the contents loose while keeping one hand around the neck of the jar to steady it. After some jiggling, she hears a pop. Whatever's inside is free. And her captor gently pulls it out for her to see.

Sierra screams with as much power as she can muster from her lungs and aching vocal cords. She does not need to ask him if the severed head he is dangling by the hair is Leah's. That she is dead is hardly a surprise. She long since figured they were looking for a body. But never in her wildest dreams did she think she would see Leah this way.

"Been keeping it on ice here. Can't very well keep it at my place, can I? Just in case you guys got a search warrant or something."

She wants to throw up in the worst way. The desire is overpowering. But there's nothing in her stomach to come out. She doesn't even have any spit in her mouth. But the worst part is the image seared in her brain. The image she knows she will never be able to scrub from her memory. That and Mitch's silly boyish grin. *He's really enjoying this!* She has to turn away and shut her eyes. *What kind of a monster does this?*

"What are you planning to do with it, have it stuffed and mounted like a deer?" she asks.

"Haven't got the time for that, honey," he says as he carefully places Leah's head back in the jar and reaches for the top.

Oh yeah, he's got cancer. Not long for this world.

"So is that what you're planning to do with me? Turn me into another trophy piece?"

"Oh no. I've got another purpose for you. But first, I've got a job to finish. The one I would have finished if you hadn't interrupted me."

Now I remember. You were up to something.

Having twisted the top back on the frosty jar, he picks it up and places it on the floor before slipping the blindfold back over her eyes. Then she feels him grab her right arm. His hand is cold. *Not surprising after he had been handling a human ice cube.* She tenses up when she feels the prick of a needle on the inside of her elbow. It stings as he drives it in. Then she feels some cold liquid being injected. Whatever it is, he must be pumping a gallon of it into her arm. Finally, he yanks the needle out.

"Time to go back to sleep," he says.

Then she passes out.

Chapter 27

The Final Showdown
Saturday, February 3, 8:11 PM

Sitting alone behind the wheel of the Impala parked at the edge of the lot, Mitch is growing increasingly impatient. And cold. Occasionally, he'll start up the engine and run the heater for a while. It makes him even more grateful that he took the Impala out there and not the delivery truck he stole the other night. *The truck felt like a goddamned icebox.* Not to mention that the cops probably have an APB out on it already. There's no way he could take it out on the road. Even if there's only a one in a million chance that some cop gets the brain wave of running the plate. He knows this is his last chance. He cannot afford to make another mistake. Nothing can be left to chance. It's why he must use the direct approach now. No more of the kind of complicated schemes Wile E. Coyote would concoct to catch the Road Runner. No Burmese tiger traps. No rocket sleds from the Acme catalog. The hell if he gets caught at this point. *What are they going to do, string me up at Portage and Main?* Whatever the consequences, he must finish this, his last and most important job. Only then can he meet his maker with a clear conscience.

He has been there for a couple of hours now, waiting for them to wind up the big shindig at Gaffer's. Where they're stuffing their faces in the banquet room and chatting about the annual kids' ice-fishing derby they took part in earlier in the day out by the nearby Lockport Bridge. Patting themselves on the back for all the money they raised for cancer research. *Oh yeah, you're so wonderful. Give yourselves a fucking gold star.* And Ben is one of them. Mitch spotted him through the binoculars. Out there on a river dredging up a catfish. Ben is a sucker for those cancer fundraisers. It's why his little half-assed company is a sponsor. He did a website for a cancer charity pro bono. The guy even wrote a book about his young friend who lost her seven-month battle with cancer. Really earned himself a lot of brownie points over that one. So Mitch didn't exactly need to put on his Sherlock hat to know he'd be there.

Inside the Impala, the temperature is falling maddeningly low once again. And the windows are fogging up. He reaches for the keys to turn it on. Keeping his fingers crossed that it will start. But then out of the corner of his eye, he spots a couple coming out. As they pass under the light, he recognizes them from the group who were out on the river. *They're not just a couple of locals who went out for dinner.* It's the first sign that the party is breaking up. And Ben is bound to be among the first to leave. Because he always is. He's a morning guy. Doesn't like to be out late at night. Mitch knows that about him. He's studied Ben's habits for years. One of his high school teachers said you could set your watch by him. So he reaches for the gun. The one the detective was carrying. She sure won't be needing it anymore. He switches off the safety catch and loads it before stepping outside.

Positioned behind the metal signpost with a clear sight line to the main entrance, Mitch watches. And waits. Seconds pass. They feel like hours. He is growing ever anxious. He is almost trembling at the prospect of Ben walking through those glass doors. It's the moment he's been dreaming of ever since getting the bad news in Dr. Hussain's office. But still no one is leaving. *Don't they want to get home? Why do they want to stay out here in the middle of nowhere and shoot the shit?* He thinks about running inside the foyer and pulling the fire alarm switch. *That would sure get them out in a big hurry.* But he knows that wouldn't work. Too many things could go wrong. Ben would just get lost in the crowd. So he has no choice but to steady himself against the post and wait in the darkness. That much he has in his favor. No one inside can possibly see him. He is perfectly sheltered from the lights on the sign, and the streetlight beaming down on the highway behind him is much too far away. Even if someone came driving by, they'd likely not spot him.

As the minutes drag on, however, he is getting increasingly cold. The light parka he's wearing isn't cutting it. Nor are his light faux leather mitts. There is a stinging pain shooting through his fingers. *That quarterback from Miami who said cold weather was a mental thing is full of shit!* For sure, now he wishes he had worn his snowmobile suit instead. He should have counted on having to spend a little time outside. But he can't turn back now. He has to stick it out. He considers going back inside the Impala to warm up for a couple of minutes. But then he spots some activity in the foyer. *Could it be?* His eyes are glued to the glass doors. Then they open. Someone steps through. *It's him! There is a God!* Mitch firms up his grip on the gun using both hands. He extends his arms and aims it toward the open door. Locking in on his target, he gently wraps his index finger around the trigger. Ready to fire as soon as he gets a clean shot. But it must be the perfect shot. He knows he will only get one chance. He watches as his target moves closer. Mitch's prayers are being answered. At last, the decisive moment is at hand. *Just one more step, you bastard . . .*

As he readies himself to pull the trigger that will send the bullet from the chamber into Ben's skull, someone shoves him on his right shoulder. There isn't much force behind it, but enough to cause him to lose his balance and awkwardly fall over on the icy asphalt, still with his right hand on the gun and his index finger wrapped around the trigger. It goes off as he lands on his backside. The sound of the blast shatters the nighttime silence. It has also shattered something in his abdominal cavity, something Mitch realizes as he looks down in horror and sees the barrel pointed directly at his midsection. Blood pours out as he doubles over in severe pain. He wails like a stuck pig and rolls over as he continues bleeding externally and internally. Despite the pain, he turns around and props himself up on his elbows in an attempt to crawl back to the Impala. He knows he has to get out of there. Otherwise, they will take him to the hospital. And then it's game over. But he can barely move. The pain consumes him. He knows this is no surface wound. Losing energy, he falls flat on his face. He tries to extend his arm out in a final desperate attempt to will himself back to the Impala. He thinks he might be able to pull himself along the ground. It's his only chance. But he is losing too much blood. He is much too weak. He cannot move. And he begins losing consciousness.

Finally, he passes out.

Chapter 28

Panic

Saturday, February 3, 8:38 PM

Petra's mind is racing a million miles an hour. Which is about the same speed she's going down Henderson Highway in her blue Honda SUV heading back to the city. She knows she's going way too fast. But she doesn't care. The faster she gets away from there, the better.

She still can't believe what happened even though she saw it with her own eyes. It was something she could never have possibly expected. It was supposed to be a nice day. Well, as nice as it can be when the high temperature for the day doesn't get above −25. Not to mention a gale-force wind blowing out of the north. Out there in the middle of nowhere, there's nothing to stop it. But the sun was shining and she had such a good feeling going up there that she even picked up a tub of ice cream at a convenience store on the way. They were out of chocolate mocha, but she settled for chocolate swirl. There was hardly anything left by the time she got there. Where she was going to see Patrick. Her Patrick. It always bothers him when she calls him Patrick. My name is Ben, he says. But he always reminds her of Patrick, her nephew. And every time she sees Ben, she can't help but think of Patrick. So she calls him Patrick.

She went up there to try to make things right with him. Told her husband she was going on an outing with the photo club. Threw her camera gear in the back just to make it look good. She was sure Patrick would be in good spirits. Not all surly like he's been lately. She knows those cancer fundraisers are near and dear to his heart. But he just blew her off. Dissed her right in front of everyone. But after going for dinner at a Chinese restaurant in Selkirk, she decided to give it one more try before heading back into the city. Hoping he'd be in a better mood following the reception. It was there that she saw that man sitting alone in his car looking squirrely. Even in the dimly lit parking lot, she could tell he was a real weirdo. She had no idea what he was up to, but she knew he was up to something even before he stepped out of the car. Then when she saw the gun, she completely freaked out. Initially she hesitated. She thought about calling 911. But there was no time for that. So she bolted out of her car and went right for him. She knew this wasn't just a robbery. He was going to shoot somebody. Maybe even Patrick. Luckily, he didn't see her coming before she pushed him to the ground. Otherwise, he might have shot her. But instead, he shot himself.

That's when she really panicked. *What if the cops think I did it?* So she pried the gun loose from his hands. Tried to wipe all the gooey blood and guts off on his coat. She doesn't know why, but she fished in his pocket and grabbed his wallet and phone too. Maybe there would be something that would connect him to her. *OK, it doesn't make sense.* So when she passed the Half Moon just a half mile out of town and saw their dumpster, she pulled over and tossed it all in there before getting back in her SUV and putting down the hammer.

As she keeps up the breakneck speed, she struggles to negotiate the many curves this highway is noted for. She crosses the double solid yellow line more than once. She slides on the ice, coming close to losing control a couple of times. Passing the curve at Bowen Avenue, she knows she's getting close to the city. And when she gets past the Perimeter Highway, she'll be able to blend in with the regular traffic. They won't be able to finger her. So she begins to calm down a little. That is until she comes up behind some old fogy crunched up right against the steering wheel of his little Volkswagen Bug, puttering along at about, like, two miles an hour. *Christ, I can get out and walk faster!* She practically has to slam on the brakes to avoid running into the back end of him. She leans on the horn. *Move it or lose it, grandpa!* But it doesn't help. If anything, he slows down even more. Probably just to spite her. She knows that just ahead around the bend is where the highway widens to two lanes right before the light at Hoddinott Road in front of Dr. F.W.L. Hamilton School. A niece of hers goes there. But she can't wait. She has to pass him now. Without checking, she swings out to her left and floors it, quickly leaving Mr. Chug-Chug in her dust. *Up yours, asshole!* It is only after flashing her tormentor a triumphant middle finger that she notices the headlights of the speeding Toyota Camry headed directly for her, its driver madly honking his horn trying to get her attention. With the Camry only two or three car lengths away, she whips the wheel to her right, avoiding a head-on collision with the Camry. However, she has made the turn much too violently. She slams on the brakes and tries swinging back the other way, but she is unable to stop from sliding along the ice and careening into a row of super mailboxes, all that separates her from the steep embankment leading straight down to the river. It is a spot she is familiar with, as it is the only one along this stretch of highway with a clear view of the river. It was just last summer, in fact, when she stopped there one evening and set up her tripod to get some shots. One of those shots even earned her a ribbon at her photo club.

The airbags deploy as her car flips over a couple of times on its way down the embankment, coming to rest upside down on the ice. She is dazed, her head having bounced off the roof like a basketball. But she is still alive and in one piece, though unaware of how little time she has before she must escape from her Honda, which is perilously perched on the edge of a small patch of open water. She immediately unhooks her seat belt once she hears the ice cracking and feels the two-ton vehicle slowly tipping into the water. As the icy river water rushes in and begins to envelop her totaled SUV, she frantically tries to push the driver-side door open, but it is jammed shut. She punches on the window with her elbow and forearm with all her might, but she cannot break the glass. *Why didn't I sign up for that weight training class?* Seconds later, she screams as the Honda falls in and begins a rapid descent to the riverbed below.

For her, it will be a one-way trip.

Chapter 29

One Last Call
Monday, February 5, 5:38 PM

Faahima has had a long day. She just wants to go home. She doesn't even want to look at the phone. It's been ringing off the hook just like it does most every day. But it has been especially bad today. It's been wearing her down. Day after day, the same thing. Yelling. Screaming. Whining. Complaining. Like it's her fault that their loved one has cancer. Or that the doctor can't cure them. Or can't see them this very instant. They think by unloading their whole life story and crying their eyes out that she can get them in to see the doctor faster. *Wait your turn like everyone else!* Maybe she'll feel better after her vacation. She's been looking forward to going back to Iran. She hasn't seen her family in a couple of years. But she knows it's only a temporary reprieve. And then it will be back to the same old shit. Right about now, she's ready to tell Dr. Hussain to take this job and shove it. It's just not worth it anymore.

At least she doesn't have to answer any more calls today. Even though the doctor is still in, running late as always seeing the last of his patients, the phones automatically go to voice mail after 5:00. So she gets up out of her chair to tidy up around the waiting room. Her last task of the day. And as usual, it looks like a war zone. Magazines and papers are strewn all over the place. There's food left on the chairs. Reaching under a table, she picks up the banana peel she's been smelling all day. *People are such pigs!* As she gets up, she notices a tattered newspaper on a chair. It's open to the big story of the day, the shooting up in Lockport over the weekend. She read about it first thing this morning. Guy was shot outside a restaurant. He was still alive when the paramedics got there, but he had lost too much blood and was pronounced dead at the hospital. Police haven't been able to identify him yet, nor have they found the gun. Her eyes then drift to the bottom of the page. There's a little write-up on a car accident on Henderson Highway not far from where the guy was shot. Some woman apparently lost control and went right into the drink. *That's what happens when you drive like a maniac. You'd think people who were born and raised here would learn how to drive on snow and ice!* After tossing the banana peel, newspapers and other junk in the bin, she returns to her desk to gather her purse and coat. But then she notices a note she left for herself. *Damn!* There's one more call to make before she leaves for the day. She doesn't even need to read the number. She's called three times already today. But Dr. Hussain wants her to keep trying. So she picks up the phone and dials. And again, all she gets is voice mail. After the beep, she leaves yet another message.

"Hello, Mr. Schubert, this is Dr. Hussain's office calling. Please call the office as soon as possible."

Once again she gives the number and hangs up. Then she shakes her head. For the life of her, she can't understand why he hasn't returned her calls.

You'd think he'd want to know there was a mix-up in pathology and his tumor is benign.

Chapter 30

Two Years Later
Saturday, April 18, 3:01 AM

The sound of little Kenny crying wakes Sierra up. She reaches over the bed, takes her son from the crib and tries to rock him back to sleep with a soft lullaby. Looking into his eyes as he begins to slowly drift off, she is again so thankful for this adorable bundle of joy. After she came out of the coma, she wanted to get rid of it right away when they told her she was pregnant. The thought of having Mitch Schubert's child growing inside her made her sick to her stomach. To this day, she can hardly bear to say the bastard's name, let alone think of how he had his way with her. But they said she was too far along. She had simply been out too long.

The coma was a natural reaction, they said. She just shut down. It was her way of dealing with the emotional trauma of what happened. She still sees a counselor. Apparently it can take years for people who are taken hostage to recover. Some never truly do. She's still recovering physically too. She still has severe headaches and there are still scars from the savage beating she took. Her face looks like it was put through a meat grinder. But at least she's alive. And only because of Ken. He was the first to notice she was missing when he went to Ben's block and found her car parked across the street. Then he traced an abandoned car left at Gaffer's, where Schubert was shot, to an address in Gimli. It was a long shot, he said, but just for the hell of it, he ran a title search of properties in the area and came up with someone in Schubert's family. *That nose of his!* If he hadn't found her, she'd have wasted away out there and died. He truly saved her life. And that of her son. So when it came time to naming the baby, it was an easy choice. Kenneth Stammers Van Gelder.

She feels a soft touch on her shoulder. It's Ron. She tried not to wake him. But she couldn't help it. That's life with a newborn. He smiles. He's been so understanding with her. And with the baby. She couldn't imagine having a better husband and father. It's why she enthusiastically supported the idea of him formally adopting Kenny. Just as she later did with his son. Lucas is wonderful. The two of them get along so well. Ron says Lucas and his mother fought like cats and dogs. She wouldn't even call him her son. To her, Lucas was just "the boy." Of course, Ron felt bad when his first wife died in a car accident. Rolled her car off an embankment into the river somewhere north of the city. Investigators said she was driving too fast and lost control on the ice. But their marriage had been falling apart long before that. It all started when Petra first went on sick leave from her job with the feds over a supposed anxiety attack. At first, Ron supported her, as a good husband should. But then he began to see it for what it was. A complete fraud. All so she could stay home and collect free money. In the last few months, she wasn't even trying to hide it anymore. A real government superstar, as someone called her.

Sierra often chuckles about how they met. In the waiting room of a law firm, of all places. *How many couples can say that?* She was there to see Cammi, while he was there to see another lawyer in regard to Petra's estate. Once they started dating, they both found it so strange that Petra's accident occurred on the same night Schubert was shot. So it was a no-brainer to hold their wedding reception at Gaffer's. They were even married in a small church nearby across the river.

Kenny quickly drifts off to dreamland once again, so Sierra puts him back in the crib before snuggling back under the covers in the hopes of getting a little more sleep. She's doing a big presentation today and needs all the rest she can get. Which hasn't been much lately. It's all part of her new job as a victim services coordinator. She absolutely loves it and it's given her a new sense of purpose, one she never had before. They did offer Sierra her old job back after the murder charge was dropped. But she knew she wasn't cut out to be a detective. And besides, there was no way she could go back. Not after the way Andrea and everyone else turned their backs on her.

Ron turns out the light on his side, then kisses her on the forehead.

"Good night, dear."

About the Author

Born and raised in Winnipeg, Manitoba, Curtis Walker lives in St. Catharines, Ontario. His passions include the history of the original Winnipeg Jets (1972-1996) and the World Hockey Association as well as the New Jersey Generals and the United States Football League.

In addition to his three books on the Jets, Curtis has written other titles. *My Journey with Carli* is the story of his friend Carli Ward, a 25-year-old who passed away of cervical cancer. *View from Section 26* features a look at minor-league hockey from his many years following the Manitoba Moose of the now-defunct IHL. He takes a politically incorrect look at his hometown in *Shattered Dreams*, a heavily sarcastic diary of a Utopian socialist who eventually sours on Winnipeg and opens his eyes to the harsh reality of socialism. A frequent bus traveler, he shares many of his experiences in *On the Bus Again*, tales from riding the buses between Winnipeg and Minneapolis, and he offers an in-depth, week-by-week history of his favorite football team in *Fallen Generals*. He details the experiences of a Web developer in a bad job that becomes a financial-services horror story in *The Contented Cows*, and *The Protector* is his first murder mystery, featuring an unlikable yet determined detective who matches wits with a diabolical and devious adversary. Finally, he chronicles the Canadian junior hockey fan experience in *Tales from the Dog Pound* and the sordid history of the National Hockey League's Atlanta Thrashers in *Broken Wings*.

Visit his website at http://curtiswalker.com/.